**"Bailey, could you trust me?" Johnny asked gently as he moved closer.**

"Yes, I think I could." She lifted her hand to his cheek, rubbing her thumb over the milk mustache he still wore on his upper lip.

It was a small gesture, but for the first time she'd voluntarily touched him. A flurry of emotions raced through him and he struggled for control.

"Then do you think you could give me a hug?" He opened his arms. She hesitated a moment, then moved into them and they closed around her.

He pulled her closer against him, inhaling the wonderful, warm, womanly scent of her. Sliding his hands up her back, he threaded his fingers through her silky hair. He meant to ask permission to kiss her, but his intention was forgotten when he met her gaze and saw his own need and desire shimmering in her eyes. . . .

## WHAT ARE *LOVESWEPT* ROMANCES?

They are stories of true romance and touching emotion. We believe those two very important ingredients are constants in our highly sensual and very believable stories in the *LOVESWEPT* line. Our goal is to give you, the reader, stories of consistently high quality that may sometimes make you laugh, sometimes make you cry, but are always fresh and creative and contain many delightful surprises within their pages.

Most romance fans read an enormous number of books. Those they truly love, they keep. Others may be traded with friends and soon forgotten. We hope that each *LOVESWEPT* romance will be a treasure—a "keeper." We will always try to publish

*LOVE STORIES YOU'LL NEVER FORGET*
*BY AUTHORS YOU'LL ALWAYS REMEMBER*

The Editors

# *Loveswept* ®603

## Theresa Gladden
## Hart's Law

BANTAM BOOKS
NEW YORK · TORONTO · LONDON · SYDNEY · AUCKLAND

HART'S LAW
*A Bantam Book / March 1993*

*If you would be interested in receiving protective vinyl*
*covers for your Loveswept books, please write to this address*
*for information:*

*Loveswept*
*Bantam Books*
*P.O. Box 985*
*Hicksville, NY 11802*

ISBN 0-553-44370-4

*Published simultaneously in the United States and Canada*

*Bantam Books are published by Bantam Books, a division of*
*Bantam Doubleday Dell Publishing Group, Inc. Its trademark,*
*consisting of the words "Bantam Books" and the portrayal of*
*a rooster, is Registered in U.S. Patent and Trademark Office*
*and in other countries. Marca Registrada. Bantam Books, 666*
*Fifth Avenue, New York, New York 10103.*

PRINTED IN THE UNITED STATES OF AMERICA

OPM        0 9 8 7 6 5 4 3 2 1

*For Jeannine and Will Wilkins*
*and*
*Chris and John Heinrich*

I would like to acknowledge the invaluable assistance given to me by the following professionals of the Rockingham County Sheriff's Department in Wentworth, North Carolina, who generously shared their time and expertise: Sheriff Bobby Vernon, Deputy Debbie Smith, Sergeant J. P. Johnson, and Captain D. W. Curry.

# One

The dispute over the dead, frozen goat had been settled. The deceased was now wrapped in a feed sack in the trunk of Sheriff Johnny Hart's police cruiser.

The weather was cranky, cranky as the two quarreling farmers Johnny had just left. Snow mixed with rain spat down, turning the stretch of unpaved country road in front of him into a slushy mud puddle.

Johnny couldn't wait to get back to Profitt to pass the buck—or in this case, the goat—to Gil, the animal-control officer. The story of how he had acquired the frozen goat might be worth the price of a beer after work at Cole Wan's Bar and Grill.

The crackling hiss of radio static interrupted his happy thoughts of beer, pretzels, and maybe a game of pool to go with them.

"County to Unit One. County to Unit One."

Johnny grabbed the cruiser's mike. "Unit One. Go ahead, County."

2 • *THERESA GLADDEN*

"Sheriff, your mama wants you to pick her up at Rhonda's House of Beauty after you get off work." The dispatcher sounded highly amused.

He suppressed a groan. "Uh, yeah . . . Affirmative, County. Ten four."

Johnny wished the daytime dispatcher, Bea Early, would use the code he'd made up to cover his mother's messages. Bea knew as well as he did that minding each other's business was the main form of winter entertainment in the rural area. He could almost hear all the nosy Parkers listening in on their police scanners—and there were quite a few in the county—slapping their knees and chuckling over how Marian Hart considered the sheriff's official vehicle her personal escort service.

"Hold your ten-four, Sheriff," the dispatcher came back. "Thought you'd want to know we got a candidate for the detective's position."

That bit of information fell into Johnny's lap like a tidbit of juicy gossip. Some local bureaucrat with a sense of humor, a bigger sense of importance, and nothing better to do, had recently decreed that the Sheriff's Department in Profitt, Ohio, ought to have an investigative unit with an experienced detective in charge. Johnny's grin grew wider. An investigative unit of *one*. It was going to be a real hoot to see who applied for that prestigious position.

"No shi—" Johnny quickly broke off and began again. "No kidding. We got us a live one. Who is it?"

"Bailey Asher."

Johnny's reaction was swift and surprising. He

almost drove the cruiser off the side of the road and into a ditch.

When he had the car back under control, he keyed the radio mike. "Did you say Bailey Asher?"

"Affirmative. Asher is a Cleveland *dick*-tective," Bea answered between electronic crackles. "She's got eight years' experience in law enforcement. The last five on the vice squad. Ten-four."

Johnny let out a low whistle as he replaced the mike. Shock wore off as nostalgia quickly took over.

Bailey Asher had been a five-year-old red-haired hellion the first time he met her. She'd come to Profitt to stay the summer with her uncle and aunt who lived next door to his family. Mad at being forced to play with a girl—which to a six-year-old boy was a fate worse than being eaten by a monster from outer space—he had made some smart remark to her about having to play with a sissy, and she had punched him in the stomach. A solid friendship had been born.

From that day on he'd looked forward to the end of the school year and Bailey's summer-long visit. The two of them had skinned their knees together, climbed trees, and played baseball and football. They'd gotten into mischief together, shared secrets, and played cops and robbers. Bailey had always insisted on being the cop, because her grandfather and her father were cops in the big city of Cleveland. She had been determined, even then, to be just like them.

The year she was thirteen, he'd been shocked to discover his best friend had been transformed into a pretty girl—a real beauty with the face of an angel, long legs, dark red hair swinging down to her waist in a braid, and feathery black lashes framing green eyes. She'd still acted the tomboy, though. Before the summer ended they had traded their first kiss.

Johnny smiled. It was the kind of fond smile that came up from the depths of a man's heart on those rare occasions when he was reminded of his first awkward attempt to kiss a girl, the first stirrings of youthful passion.

The summer Bailey had turned seventeen, he'd taken one look at her and his heart had started beating so hard, he'd thought it would explode. June, July, and August, for three of the best months of his life she had been his best friend, his girlfriend, and the innocent recipient of long, thorough lessons in the art of kissing.

That was the last time they'd been together. They had both gone on to college in different cities with promises to write and keep in touch, promises that had gradually faded and ceased altogether, as such things do. In the thirteen years since, the only news he'd had of Bailey had been bits and pieces garnered from her now-widowed aunt, who still lived next door to his parents.

Johnny drew in a deep breath. "Well, I'll be damned," he said, slowly releasing the air from his lungs. "Bailey's coming back to town."

The notion of seeing her again intrigued him more than a little. He was also damned curious. According to her aunt, Bailey had a very successful career.

Why would she be seeking a job with a modest Sheriff's Department like his in a sparsely populated area like Chatham County?

• • •

At ten o'clock that evening Bailey Asher stood ankle-deep in dirty snow on the corner of a Cleveland waterfront street. The cold, damp January wind coming off Lake Erie seeped through her tight jeans, black boots, and leather jacket.

Her backup team of three undercover police officers were all in position. She glanced toward the dark mouth of a parking lot where her partner, Charlie, was wired to relay her signals to the rest of the team. He was playing his street-scavenger role to the hilt, muttering and singing to himself in a low, raspy voice as he delved through the contents of a Dumpster.

Bailey's attention was drawn to a white van slowly cruising toward her. She'd seen it circle the block several times. It pulled up beside her. The passenger window slid down.

Vans were dangerous. It was impossible to tell who, how many, and what was inside. She knew she should shake her head and refuse to approach the vehicle. But something she'd noticed about it made her paste on a smile and saunter over to the curb.

"Hi!" Her gaze swept the van's interior. Single occupant. A man in his mid-forties. He wore a plain gold wedding band on the ring finger of his left hand. Another cheating husband. She wanted to puke. Instead, she kept smiling.

"Are you *dating*?" He looked her over with blatant interest.

"I'm not out here freezing my buns off for nothing. What'd you have in mind?"

"Everything, honey. How much?"

She told him.

He didn't argue.

Bailey ran her fingers through her short russet hair. The gesture was a prearranged signal that the violation had been made. She opened the door and climbed into the van.

Minutes later, behind a designated apartment building, Bailey and the team of undercover vice officers took the would-be customer into custody. He was charged with soliciting an act of prostitution.

Shortly after the arrest, Bailey headed back to the waterfront street with Charlie. The second they were out of sight of the others, her partner said, "Geez, kid! You got a death wish or something?"

Bailey glanced at Charlie's sharp profile. She felt a lecture coming on. "Only on Tuesdays." Her attempt at humor was strained, as strained as her smile.

"It ain't Tuesday. Why the hell did you get into that van?" The concern buried beneath his annoyed tone made Bailey feel a twinge of guilt. "You know there could have been six doped-up guys armed to the eyeballs with Saturday night specials and machine guns in there."

"There was a 'Baby on Board' sign in the back window." It was a poor excuse for ignoring the rules, and she knew it.

"So you decided it was safe?" he asked, his voice incredulous.

She shrugged. "Sure."

"Dumb, kid. Real dumb." He stopped beneath the street light at the corner and faced her. The scowl on his face was enough to make any wrong-doer quake. It didn't intimidate Bailey at all.

"Nothing happened. It was a good bust."

"You're lucky we're not picking up pieces of you off the sidewalk."

Bailey gave a quick, unladylike snort.

Charlie countered with a concise four-letter word. "Do me a favor, kid. Stay outta vans. I for damn sure don't want your dad and brothers beating the crap out of me for letting you get yourself killed."

"That would definitely be a fate I wouldn't wish on my worst enemy." She relented, holding up her hands. "Okay. You're right. I'm sorry."

Charlie eyed her speculatively. "What's the matter with you? You've been acting weird lately. I'm beginning to think you aren't pumped up about the job anymore."

He was too close to the truth for comfort. Bailey fussed with the collar of her jacket, taking her time before answering. "Nothing's wrong. I'm just going through the birthday blahs. You know what I mean."

"Cheer up, birthday girl. The big three-oh isn't so bad." He grinned. "A new sports car and a blonde with big boobs perked me right up when I reached forty last year. Go buy yourself a jazzy little automobile. Make it candy-apple red to match your hair and your temper. Better yet, deflate a few of the birthday condoms we gave you and get laid. You'll feel better."

Bailey laughed. Earlier in the evening the team had surprised her with a cake and a bouquet of thirty colorful condoms blown up like balloons. "You're a pig, Charlie."

"True. I sure smell like one right now. Speaking of smelly things, I've got a hot date with a trash bin." He left her and headed toward his post. "Stay out of vans and watch your backside, kid."

"You're supposed to be watching my backside."

"And a nice one it is too," he yelled back.

As soon as she was alone, weariness and depression settled over Bailey. She wished the night were over. Wished herself anyplace but where she was.

She sighed and warmed her cupped hands with her breath. She felt bad for lying about having the birthday blahs and for scaring Charlie by getting into the van. He'd been right to reprimand her. She'd taken an unnecessary risk simply because the Baby on Board sign had ticked her off.

It wasn't as though she weren't accustomed to seeing wedding rings and even baby car seats belonging to the men she arrested. Years of working vice had made her shock-proof. What bothered her was that she was no longer shocked by such things.

She was even more concerned that her attitude toward men in general had changed. She tended to automatically assume the worst about them, and she had stopped dating altogether eleven months ago.

Disillusioned. Dissatisfied. That was how she felt about the male species, about herself, and especially about her job.

Bailey knew she had to get off the streets. Unfortunately, her boss considered her too valuable right where she was—using her body as bait instead of her brain. As long as she remained with the department, she was certain she'd be stuck indefinitely working prostitution, pandering, and infiltrating illegal enterprises that were off-limits to men.

She was too ambitious to settle for that. Since her options were limited where she was, she was determined to create her own options.

Thanks to her aunt Cookie, Bailey had heard about an opening with the Sheriff's Department in Profitt. Heading up a rural-county investigative unit would be her first stepping-stone to better opportunities.

Living in a rural county wasn't going to be easy for her. Profitt, Chatham County's largest town with three thousand residents, was about as small and rustic as towns got in central Ohio. It wasn't even a whistle-stop on the much-traveled route between Cincinnati and Cleveland.

Aunt Cookie had invited her to live with her, though, if the job panned out. Being with Cookie, who had been more mother than aunt to her, would be a pleasure and would make a temporary career move to the country more bearable.

Her mind circled around to Johnny Hart. Before she'd heard about the job, she'd hardly spared her old friend a thought in a very long time. What little she'd heard about him over the years had been gleaned from Cookie. His name had cropped up in conversations with Cookie more often of late, since her widowed aunt had started keeping company with Harry Baskin, Johnny's uncle.

Now that she knew she'd be seeing Johnny again, that he'd be interviewing her, memories of her childhood friend kept creeping out of the shadows of her mind.

At age six Johnny had been a skinny but sturdy

little boy with big, sleepy brown eyes and an engaging gap-toothed grin. Twenty-five years later Bailey simply couldn't picture him as the sheriff of his hometown. Law enforcement was the last profession on earth she would have expected him to pursue. The boy she'd known had been much too easygoing and tenderhearted for such work.

A gifted athlete all through his youth, Johnny had had his ambition firmly centered on playing professional football. She couldn't help wondering what had happened to change his mind and what had launched him into a profession his personality seemed so unsuited for.

The thought of seeing him again unsettled her. Perhaps it was just a natural reaction to the notion of working closely with someone she'd explored the mysteries of kissing with at age thirteen. She vividly recalled the experience. They had both felt so silly and awkward, they hadn't tried it again until four years later. And what a long, hot summer that last summer had been!

Worry slid into her stomach and formed a painful knot. She hoped Johnny didn't remember a thing about that last summer.

Bailey shoved her personal thoughts aside as a sleek Mercedes inched past her. The automobile rolled to a stop several yards away, then backed up.

*Happy damn birthday.*

With a sigh of resignation Bailey put on a smile and went over to make her fourth bust of the night.

The job in Profitt was looking better by the minute.

# Two

The Chatham County Sheriff's Department seemed awfully quiet and deserted for a Friday morning. The only sound Bailey heard was the hollow echo of her heels on the dingy tile of the corridor.

She caught herself humming the theme to *The Twilight Zone* as she peered into various doorways in her hunt for the sheriff's office. A bored-looking female dispatcher with an amazing thatch of bleached hair sat in the Communications Center. The Records Department had a single occupant, a young male deputy busy eating a doughnut while scribbling on a yellow legal pad. A lounge area and conference room were both deserted.

"Well, I wanted a change of pace," she murmured. And the pace here was as different from a busy city precinct house as it could get and still be considered in the same business of law enforcement.

Trying not to be disappointed by the smallness of the facility and its lack of personnel and busi-

*11*

ness, she walked on until she came to a door marked SHERIFF'S OFFICE. She entered and found herself in a small reception area. No one sat at the administrative assistant's desk.

Bailey took a moment to quell the butterfly herd in her stomach before announcing her arrival to the sheriff. She told herself it was ridiculous to feel so nervous about seeing Johnny Hart again. Inhaling a deep breath, she rapped lightly on his closed door. Hearing a muffled "Come in," she let herself into the office.

He was sitting in a high-backed swivel chair behind his desk, listening to someone on the phone. He gave her a singularly attractive smile and motioned her inside.

His preoccupation allowed her to study him. In the years since she'd seen him, Johnny Hart had acquired a real man's body. Tall, lean, and firmly muscled, he looked damn fine in a uniform.

Beyond a few laugh lines around his eyes, his face looked the same, with dark arching brows and a long blade of a nose, slightly crooked from a long-ago football injury. His smile made his face come alive with humor and character, instantly diluting the impression of laziness given by the sleepy expression in his heavy-lidded brown eyes.

Still wavy and thick, his brown hair was shorter on the sides and slightly longer in the front. And he was sporting sexy sideburns these days, she noticed with faint amusement.

He glanced her way and grinned. Embarrassed to be caught staring at him, she walked over to examine a collection of framed prints decorating one wall. Each print depicted a law officer from the Wild West era.

"Bailey?"

The warmth infused into her name by that deep, rich voice shook her composure for a second. She regained her poise and turned to face him. "Hello."

He rose to his feet. "Hot damn, Bailey! It's good to see you." He started across the room, his arms stretched out as though to snatch her up in a bear hug the second he reached her.

She quickly held out her right hand, hoping he would get the hint. "It's nice to see you again, Sheriff Hart."

He looked down at her hand, up at her face, then let his arms drop to his sides. "What's this 'Sheriff Hart' stuff?" He gripped her hand in a firm, warm handshake. "You used to call me Johnny."

She couldn't help but return his grin. Maybe this interview wasn't going to be as tough as she'd feared. "I used to call you a lot of things."

"'Toad face' was one of the few repeatable ones."

She laughed. "That's true."

Johnny felt a bemused smile coming on as his gaze roved over her. He couldn't recall ever having seen a woman except Bailey with skin so smooth and milky white, and eyes the color of ripe limes.

"I've spent the last week," he said, "imagining what you'd look like all grown up. My imagination didn't do you justice. You look good, brat."

Pink stained her cheeks. "Thank you."

"You finally tamed your wild hair." He lifted his hand to touch a silky lock of her long bangs. The short, windswept style was a perfect foil for her heart-shaped face, snippy little nose, and stubborn chin.

She looked flustered for a moment, then regained her poise. "I cut it. Anything else you want to comment on before we get this interview off the ground?"

"You're still skinny," he said, taking another poke at her temper. She was thin, but she was also gently rounded in all the places he liked.

"Thanks a lot," she answered dryly.

"How 'bout giving an old toad a hug?"

Bailey hesitated. It had been quite a while since she'd been comfortable being hugged by a man.

"Wondering if hugging one's potential boss is a breach of professional etiquette?" he asked.

She nodded. That was as good a reason as any.

"I'm the sheriff, and I get to make the rules." He grinned. "Hugging an old friend is allowed."

Amusement overcame her reluctance. "In that case I guess it would be okay."

The moment she moved into his embrace, she decided she'd made a mistake. Time just seemed to slip away. Everything flashed through her memory, from the way she once loved to rest her head upon his broad shoulder to the sizzling kisses of their youth.

She tilted her head back and met his gaze. Something stirred inside her that she hadn't felt for a very long time. It frightened her. It made her mad. She wasn't a giddy teenager anymore.

Lost in his own flood of memories and in the pleasant surprise of a new attraction mingling with the old, it took Johnny a few moments to realize her body had stiffened. And she was looking at him so warily.

"It's been a long time, brat," he said, hoping to put her at ease. "I'm a head taller than you now.

We were both five-nine the last time I saw you. I grew. You didn't, shorty." It worked. He felt her relax against him.

"That's true," she said. "Now you're a giant toad."

He had missed her, he realized with a sudden thump of his heart. He tamed the impulse to plant a kiss on her full lips, settling instead for a quick peck on her cheek.

Bailey jerked away. From his puzzled expression she knew he didn't know what to make of her abrupt reaction.

"That's no way to conduct an interview, Sheriff Hart," she said, taking a step back. She sounded priggish, even a little insulting, but it was necessary to her to put some distance between them. "Is it your policy to hug and kiss all potential employees?"

Johnny started to say, "Just the pretty ones," and thought better of it. "Nope. Just old and very dear friends like you. The Bailey I used to know didn't stand on formality."

She averted her gaze. "I'm not here to renew old friendships. Shall we get down to business?"

He watched her walk briskly to a chair beside his desk. She sat down and smoothed her straight knee-length skirt into place.

Johnny swallowed a sigh. Their reunion wasn't getting off to a good start. He took his seat behind his desk.

"So, how are you, Bailey?"

"Fine. I can't believe you're the sheriff of Chatham County. How in the world did that happen?" She frowned as though she hadn't meant or wanted to ask him anything personal.

"I didn't want to be a farmer, and I didn't want to sell insurance with my dad." He shrugged. "So I ran for sheriff. Surprised the heck out of me when I won the first election." He gave her a crooked smile. "I'm sorry if I offended you with that little kiss. Guess I was just glad to see you after all these years."

"I wasn't offended. We are old friends. It just seems inappropriate to—" She broke off. "Forget it. No harm done. However, I do feel it's best that we both keep in mind the reason I'm here today."

"We can try," he said good-naturedly. However, he truly doubted he could carry it off. Something about her tugged at his heart, something that made him want to dig beneath the cool indifference she seemed determined to maintain.

"But it won't be easy," he continued. "I've got a feeling you're going to be trouble."

Her eyes widened. "I beg your pardon?"

Their gazes met and warred with each other for a silent moment. His was curious and probing. Hers was questioning and uncertain.

Johnny wasn't usually given to speaking before thinking, but Bailey was playing havoc with his emotions. He decided he might as well speak his mind now and worry about the consequences later. "I'm attracted to you on a personal level. Unfortunately, I get the feeling that displeases you as much as it pleases me. What do you think about that?"

She looked stunned. "If you're only interested in coming on to me, I think I'd better leave," she said in a tight voice as she stood up.

He shook his head. "I wasn't coming on to you.

Just stating the truth as I see it. So don't leave. Please, sit down."

"Maybe this is a mistake. I really should go."

"If you want to. I wish you wouldn't."

He smiled at her, and that smile got to Bailey. It could have melted steel. The man was full of charm, and he knew it, she thought as she settled back into the chair.

"Let's keep personal feelings out of this," she said.

"Like it or not, I am attracted to you," he said, obviously undaunted. "I'm looking forward to getting to know you again. The job with the department is another matter entirely. Rest assured, my personal feelings will not be involved in the decision to hire you."

She gave him a cool stare. "I wouldn't look forward to getting to know me again if I were you. I'm not as sweet as I used to be."

He threw back his head and laughed. "Bailey, you were never sweet," he said when he got himself under control. "But I liked you anyway. And I think I'm going to like you a whole lot more now."

She shook her head and gave up trying to maintain a professional and emotional distance. "You're still the biggest tease in Profitt, Johnny Hart."

"And you're still the prettiest girl ever to set foot in Profitt."

"Woman," she corrected him. "I'm not a girl anymore."

He chuckled. "Same old Bailey. Nothing intimidates you. Even when you were a little thing, you had more than your share of brass and bravado."

Her lips curved around a smile. "Were you trying to intimidate me?"

He shook his head. "I never employ intimidation tactics. It's too much work. I was simply stating a fact. You were a girl the last time I saw you. If I remember correctly, it was the night we drove over to the cemetery, climbed into the backseat of my daddy's old black Chevy, and indulged in some serious kissing."

Bailey hid an exasperated smile. "Do you want to know what I remember about that night?" He nodded. "The sheriff bushwhacking us. He sneaked up to the car and shined a flashlight the size of a Hollywood spotlight right into our eyes. Scared me to death."

"That was Sheriff Rhodes. I think he used to get his jollies peeking into parked cars."

"I'll never forget the lecture he gave us," she continued. "He followed us back to my aunt Cookie's house to make sure we stayed out of trouble. Is the cemetery still the favorite teenage make-out place?"

"Where else would they go? As you probably noticed, Profitt hasn't changed all that much since the last time you were here. The Crown Theater only shows one movie on the weekends, and Bob's Drive-In stops serving promptly at ten every night."

"I noticed. Have you taken up bushwhacking duty?"

"Nope." He grinned sheepishly. "I don't have the heart to bushwhack the kids myself. So I send my deputies over there every so often to run 'em off."

"The ability to delegate is an admirable quality in a leader," she said, tongue-in-cheek.

"My philosophy exactly. How long are you planning on being in town?"

"Until tomorrow morning." She folded her hands in her lap, forcing herself to sit still and hold up her end of the idle chitchat. "I'm spending the night with Aunt Cookie."

"That's nice. My parents said to give you their best. They've gone up to Columbus to visit friends for a couple of days."

"I'm sorry to miss them. Please give them my regards."

Johnny took advantage of a moment's companionable silence to study Bailey. Her bearing and navy power suit projected confidence. The tailored look of authority was softened only by a pink silk blouse.

"Where's your coat and purse?" he asked, noticing for the first time she'd brought neither of those items into his office.

"I hate carrying a coat around, so I locked it in the trunk of my car. I don't carry a purse."

He arched an eyebrow in surprise. "Why not? Most women I know wouldn't dream of leaving home without one packed solidly with feminine doodads."

"Well, if you must know, I don't carry one because it fosters the nurturing female image."

He frowned. "I don't get it. Explain."

Bailey wished she'd kept her mouth shut. "Okay, let's say you're having lunch with two men and one woman. You have a headache. You ask one of them if they have an aspirin. Which one would it be?"

"The woman."

"Why?"

"Because the woman is more likely to have aspirins with her than a man."

She folded her arms and smiled smugly. "Right. That's the nurturing female image, the 'Mommy syndrome.' I only carry a purse if I need it to hold a weapon."

"Okay," he said, thinking it over. "You work in a profession that's predominantly male, and you want to be perceived as an equal, not a fixer and caretaker. Makes sense to me."

"You got it." Her gaze strayed to the framed sampler hanging on the wall behind him. "'Hart's Law in *cross-stitch*?" She shot him an amused look.

Johnny bit back a groan.

"Is that your version of the Ten Commandments?" She leaned forward and began reading aloud, "Thou shalt be visible in the community. Thou shalt set a good example. Thou shalt be nice. Thou shalt use common sense. Thou shalt not talk down to people. Thou shalt not give people the runaround. Thou shalt—'"

"'Have a heart,'" he interrupted, skipping down to Hart's Law number ten. "And give the sheriff a break."

Bailey cracked up at the sheepish grin on his face.

"My mother is responsible for that," he went on. "When I first took office, I guess she wrote down all my little words of wisdom and cross-stitched them for posterity." He shrugged. "She was so proud of it, how could I refuse to hang it on the wall?"

Bailey couldn't help smiling. A thirty-one-year-old man who was nice to his mother and considerate of her feelings couldn't be all bad. "I'm sorry I laughed, Johnny. Actually, I think they're good common-sense rules."

"Thank you." His smile was as warm and intimate as a kiss. "Do you want to go to lunch later? The Market Street Café has a great deluxe lunch special for three ninety-five. Meat loaf, creamed potatoes, all kinds of vegetables, hot rolls, and banana cream pie for dessert."

"No, I don't think so. Johnny—"

"Bob's Drive-In," he eagerly suggested. "They still serve the best curly fries and soft ice cream in the state. You used to love their curly fries. Bob doesn't own the drive-in anymore, though. Sold it to Greg—"

"Johnny, please!" She waved her hand to stop him. The chitchat had depleted her limited supply of patience. "I don't want to go to lunch. I *want* to discuss the job. That's the reason I'm here, remember?"

Johnny leaned back as he saw the gleam of restlessness in Bailey's eyes. That gleam was all too familiar. She was anxious to get down to business, and she wouldn't be put off any longer.

Usually, he took the most direct route in dealing with people. He wasn't the kind of man who avoided sticky issues with a lot of fancy dancing and fast talk. Unfortunately, there was no way he could make the job sound more appealing than it was. Once he laid all the cards on the table, he was afraid the interview would quickly terminate. She'd walk out, and that would be that.

He sighed. "All right. I'm impressed with your credentials, Bailey."

"Thank you." The restlessness in her eyes was instantly replaced with anticipation.

He swallowed another sigh and kept going. "According to your file and letters of recommendation, you're a prime example of a female vice officer. When you were a kid, you always said you wanted to be on the cutting edge of big-city law enforcement. Looks like you accomplished what you set out to do. Captain Asher must be real proud of you."

"I hope so." Some emotion flickered across her face and was quickly controlled.

"I understand your brothers followed in your father's footsteps too."

"Yes. Daryl is a state trooper. Ben just made lieutenant with the Homicide Division." She shot him an impatient look. "What are you looking for in an applicant?"

"One who is neatly groomed." He grinned. "I'd say you're neatly groomed. Pleasant, congenial personality, and an even temperament. You'd have to work on that." He ignored the warning glare she gave him. "Physical fitness. You look fit to me. How's your vision and hearing?"

"My vision is twenty-twenty and I can hear B.S. a mile away."

"Good." He checked a grin. "I require all my deputies to be honest and have a healthy dose of common sense. Communication skills are important." He paused and ran his gaze over her. "It's too bad you're not married. I like—"

"Married women?" she interrupted harshly. "Do you come on to married women too?"

"What?" His brows drew together in confusion.

"Just minutes ago you said you were attracted

to me. Would you have kept that information to yourself if I were married? Or would you have come on to me anyway?"

"I don't believe this." He crossed his arms over his chest and returned her icy stare. "As I was about to say before I was so *rudely* interrupted, I like my deputies to be married. Makes 'em more settled and responsible on the job. It has nothing to do with my personal preferences."

Bailey's smile was thin, without humor. "*You're* not married," she said.

He arched his brows. "Do as I say and not as I do? And just to set the record straight, I don't hit on married ladies."

"Cut to the chase. Tell me about the job."

Johnny nodded reluctantly. It was the thought of her going back to Cleveland for good that kept him dragging his feet. The second she'd walked into his office, he'd felt a raw possessiveness toward her. He'd never felt that way about a woman before, and it didn't seem to make a bit of difference when he told himself he shouldn't feel so strongly about a woman he hadn't seen in thirteen years.

"There isn't much excitement in the way of crime around here." He tipped his chair back, and it protested the movement with a loud creak. "That's fine by me. I like the work. I like dealing with people, and I like that every day is always different. But I'm not sure our sedate pace would suit you."

She pressed her lips together as though to keep from commenting. Her eyes never left his for a second.

"Rural law enforcement is a whole different ball

game," he continued, bringing his fingers together to make a steeple. "We're more integrated into the community we serve than our urban counterparts. The volume and seriousness of rural crime rarely merits specialized personnel and sophisticated equipment. It just isn't cost-effective. We spend most of our time providing services. Every officer is expected to be able to handle every call that comes in, and I expect them to display sensitivity to the true character of the community."

"I understand that open spaces are a primary problem." Her tone of voice said she was eager to let him know she wasn't totally ignorant on the subject.

"You've done your homework." He smiled with approval. "We are responsible for patrolling large expanses of area and road. That can slow response time to calls. Another problem is that handguns are owned at disproportionately higher rates in rural areas."

"How many road deputies do you employ?"

"Five. Three on day shift and two at night."

Bailey frowned. "So they're more likely to approach dangerous situations alone, and less likely to be able to count on immediate support from fellow officers."

He nodded. "But we haven't lost one yet, I'm happy to say. Like I said before, it's generally pretty quiet around here."

"What kind of cases do you handle?"

He cocked his head to one side. "Oh, mostly all we do is execute court orders, keep the peace, mind the jail, and transport prisoners." He scooped up a paper clip from his desk and began bending it out of shape. "A little larceny, an occasional Saturday night fight at Cole Wan's Bar and Grill, childish pranks, and minor domestic disturbances."

He shrugged. "That's about as exciting as it gets. I imagine you're used to a lot of action and excitement working undercover vice in the big city."

It sounded to Bailey as though he was trying to discourage her. Or was he subtly telling her he didn't think she fit the profile of a small-town peace officer? The Johnny she remembered hadn't had a subtle bone in his body, but maybe he'd grown one as he matured.

"What about murders?" she asked.

"We haven't had a murder since I took office. We don't count the time Harry Baskin murdered Jasmine."

Bailey was stunned speechless for a moment. Then she gasped, "Your uncle *killed* someone? My God, my aunt is seeing him!"

Johnny nodded. "Your aunt was real support-ive. She stuck by Harry through the whole thing. Of course, she didn't condone his actions the way some folks did. Harry had quite a cheering section in court." He flipped the twisted paper clip into his wastebasket.

"That's terrible!"

"Well, some folks thought Jasmine had it com-ing." Johnny could barely keep a straight face. "Apparently, she wasn't too popular in the neighborhood. Harry got tired of her doing her business on his doorstep and let her have it with a BB gun. Technically, that poodle died of fright, but she was dead just the same."

Bailey closed her eyes briefly in amused annoyance. "You set me up, dammit."

"Had you going for a minute, didn't I?"

She grimaced. "I remember Mr. Baskin very well. He used to call me 'girlie.' I always suspected he was a latent criminal. But I pictured him more as a con man than a canine killer. Did you have to toss him into the slammer?"

"Sure did. Judge Wilkins had been waiting for years to throw the book at Harry for being such a nuisance in the courtroom. He sentenced him to pay a hefty fine and put him on probation." A grin slid across his mouth. "Harry isn't allowed to frighten another mutt to death with malicious intent for at least two years."

Her laugh sparked an erotic hookup in Johnny's brain. She was getting under his skin faster than any woman ever had. It was a shame she'd be running back to Cleveland when he finally got around to telling her the truth.

"I understand your uncle retired from his law practice." She crossed one long, slim leg over the other, and that unconsciously feminine movement raised Johnny's blood pressure.

"Last spring," he said. "Some say Harry never knew a tort from a tart, but his clients loved him. They wept when he gave up his practice. Judge Wilkins celebrated for three days."

Bailey didn't respond to his humor because she saw the way he was staring at her legs. She uncrossed them and sat up straight with her knees pressed primly together.

"How large an operation do you have here?" she asked, firmly guiding the conversation back to impersonal ground.

His gaze returned to her face. "A small one. I take it you met the dispatcher and Deputy Evans in the Records Department?"

"I didn't exactly meet them, but go on."

"There's also a jailer and two bailiffs on duty in the small-claims courtrooms. If a bomb exploded in the building right now, it would wipe out a fourth of our manpower." He paused and waited for her reaction.

"No wonder the place looked deserted when I came in. Is it always this quiet on a weekday morning?"

"No, not always. Things have been a little slow lately. I mentioned the five road deputies, I believe. Add another jailer, one animal-control officer, a night dispatcher, and an administrative assistant—she's home taking care of a sick child today—and that's it. We work two twelve-hour shifts. I'm on call twenty-four hours a day, seven days a week. Any questions?"

"What about the Investigative Unit?" she asked, looking faintly puzzled.

"What investigative unit?"

"Are you telling me there isn't one?" Her voice came out cold, the words clipped.

"You got it. The fact is, we don't have much for an investigator to investigate."

The truth was out. Johnny sat back and waited for the fireworks to begin.

# *Three*

The fireworks didn't materialize. Bailey merely looked resigned and said, "My understanding was that I would be the detective in charge of such a unit."

Johnny felt a twinge of remorse. "You'd be in charge, of course. Of yourself. Answerable to me as the duly elected sheriff of the county."

"I don't understand." Her hands twisted together in her lap. "If you don't need an investigative detective, why are you hiring one?"

He wished she had ripped him apart verbally the way he had expected. "Local politics. The county commissioners decided we ought to have one and dug up the funding for the position. I'm sorry to have wasted your time, Bailey. I should have had my administrative assistant explain all this to you on the phone, when she called you to set up the interview."

"Why didn't you?" There was a hint of angry rebuke in her voice.

"The truth is, I was curious to see you after all these years. I wouldn't blame you if you wanted to nail my hide to the nearest barn door."

"As tempting as that sounds, I think I'll pass." She stared down at her lap for a long moment. When she looked up, she smiled as though she'd reached a decision. "I'm a good cop. Hire me to start up your new investigative unit."

"You're still interested?" Johnny was torn between astonishment and amusement.

"Yes."

"You can't be serious."

"Why not?"

"I feel compelled to point out that you're so overqualified for the job, it's ridiculous. You'd hate the slow pace. You wouldn't last a week."

Her chin went up. "You want to bet?"

"Hell no," he said, frowning. "You'd stick around just to prove me wrong. Look, Bailey, as much as I would love to have an officer of your caliber on my staff, I feel honor-bound not to raise your expectations. Rapes, grand theft, and murders are few and far between, thank heaven. You'd be assigned to respond to routine calls just like my other deputies. We're talking trespassing, hunting violations, domestic disputes, serving subpoenas and bench warrants."

Bailey met his gaze with determination. She wanted the job, and she was going to get it. Until that moment she hadn't fully understood how deep her desperation ran. Anything, *anything*, was better than going back out on the street to bust pimps, hookers, and cheating husbands.

"Johnny, I applied for the job knowing the caseload and duties would be very different from what I'm accustomed to," she said calmly, firmly. "My interest lies in widening my law-enforcement experience."

Johnny admired her poise. He wondered if he should tell her that her duties could very well include mediating disputes over dead frozen goats.

"I'm not trying to discourage you," he said, deciding not to bring up the subject of deceased goats. "I just want to give you a realistic description of what we deal with on a day-to-day basis. There's no personnel for you to supervise, no state-of-the-art equipment, no crime lab. The kind of cases we investigate rarely merit more than a few lines of newspaper type. No fame. No glory."

"I'm not after fame and glory," she said vehemently.

"What are you after, Bailey?" He tipped his chair back and watched her from half-shuttered eyes. "Ever since I heard you were applying for the job, I've been asking myself the same question over and over. Why would a law-enforcement officer with your background and experience willingly chuck a successful career to work here for me? The cut in pay alone is enough to make anyone think twice."

Bailey went still. That was it. That was the question she had been dreading, the one she'd used up her quota of patience waiting for him to ask. Maybe it was foolish, but her pride simply wouldn't allow her to tell him the real reason she'd applied for the job. The last thing she wanted to admit to Johnny Hart was that her *successful* law-enforcement career was built on her ability to masquerade as a cheap slut.

She returned his deceptively lazy smile with a cool one. "Maybe what I'm really after is *your* job."

His sleepy expression vanished, and she was pleased to see that he couldn't have been more surprised than if she'd slugged him. He sat forward quickly, making his chair give off a loud, satisfying creak.

The corners of his mouth twitched. Slowly, a grin overtook his features. The grin widened until he threw back his head and laughed.

"What's the matter, Sheriff?" she asked. "Don't you think I could do your job?"

Still chuckling softly, he rose and walked around his desk to stand in front of her. "Honey, if you want my job, I say go for it." He took hold of her arms and hauled her to her feet.

She tilted her head back and gave him a quelling glance. "I'll make a deal with you. I won't run against you for sheriff in the next election, and you won't *ever* call me 'honey.'"

In the green fire burning in her eyes, Johnny saw the girl he remembered. He smiled. "You drive a hard bargain."

"Do you mind letting go of me now?"

He minded, but he released her anyway. "I'll tell you what we're going to do," he said softly. "We're going to take a little tour of the facility, then I'm going to buy you the special deluxe lunch at the Market Street Café." He turned and started toward the door.

"What about the job?" she asked, not moving. "Do you intend to hire me?"

He glanced at her over his shoulder. "Make decisions in haste and repent in leisure."

She rolled her eyes. "Oh, please. Give me a break, not clichés."

He turned around. "Whether you realize it or not, I am giving you a break. We're both going to sleep on it." His tone of voice was gentle but firm. "We'll talk about it in the morning. That is, if you're still determined to work for me."

Bailey gritted her teeth and followed him out of the office.


Three hours later Bailey was perched on a stool at the breakfast bar in her aunt's home, watching Cookie move efficiently around the kitchen. The room was warm, cozy, and filled with the heavenly aroma of chocolate.

Cookie Hoover was in her mid-sixties, though her trim figure and smooth skin made her look younger. She was fashionably dressed in black leggings and a long, loose mint-green sweater. Her thick hair was a beautiful shade of silvery blond, compliments of Miss Clairol and the efforts of the best beautician at Rhonda's House of Beauty. She possessed the elegance of another era and the savvy of today, which Bailey admired tremendously.

"Sleep on it," Bailey muttered for the third time in as many minutes. "Did I tell you that rotten Johnny Hart said we should *sleep on it* before making a final decision?"

"Yes, dear, you did." Her aunt's mellow voice held a hint of amusement. "Johnny doesn't rush into anything."

Bailey rolled her eyes. "You mean he's slow and plodding and totally unreasonable."

Cookie looked up from arranging freshly baked brownies on a plate. "Now you know that's not true. He just likes to think things over carefully."

"Either I've got the job or not. *Sleeping* on it isn't going to change my mind. I wouldn't have applied for the blasted job if I didn't want it."

A little smile tilted the corners of Cookie's mouth. "Are you worried he won't hire you?"

"He'd be crazy to pass up someone with my background and experience." But she was afraid he might.

"Then what are you fretting about?"

Bailey got up and went to the refrigerator. "I can't stand this waiting game he's forcing me to play." She took a can of diet cola out of the fridge and popped the top. "I'm an adult. I know what I want."

"Of course you do." Her aunt came over and gently caressed her cheek. "You always did know exactly what you wanted. Tomorrow morning, you'll accept the job. Case closed. Did I tell you how happy I am to have you here?"

Bailey hugged her. "I love you." How nice it was to see the emotion that filled her heart reflected in her aunt's eyes. "I'm happy to be here too. Let's pig out."

Cookie headed for the plate of brownies. "I put in a ton of chocolate chips."

Bailey grinned. Her aunt's answer to stress was food, and plying Bailey with her favorite chocolate confection was her way of showing she loved her.

The two women sat down at the table with the plate of warm brownies between them.

"I still can't believe *he's* the sheriff," Bailey said. "I was the one who always wanted to be a cop." She bit into a melt-in-the-mouth brownie, savoring the burst of chocolate on her tongue.

Cookie smiled. "I wish you could have seen Marian Hart campaigning for him the first time he ran for office. You know she's always had her finger stuck in every civic pie. With her energy and enthusiasm she just about drove every volunteer and voter to drink at Cole Wan's. Marian was determined her boy was going to be sheriff, and that was that."

"What's Marian doing with her immense leisure hours now that she's retired from teaching?" Bailey broke off another piece of brownie and popped it into her mouth.

"Sticking her fingers in more civic pies and driving Frank crazy by scheduling *his* retirement activities down to the minute. Marian's one tireless organizer."

"They make an odd couple, don't they? Frank's the sweetest, most easygoing man."

Cookie snagged Bailey's can of diet cola and took a sip. "They're good for each other. She keeps him from turning into an old couch potato who'd do nothing but watch sports day and night, and he keeps her feet firmly anchored on the ground."

Bailey smiled. Johnny had inherited his father's temperament along with a healthy dose of sports fanaticism. "Why didn't Johnny go into professional football? Going pro was all he ever talked about when he was a kid. I thought he'd be playing until his knees gave out. Then he'd coach or something."

"I don't know," her aunt said, shrugging. "I

don't think anyone really knows why he didn't. He won statewide recognition as an outstanding player in college. The whole town thought he'd go all the way to a shining pro career. Marian told me that Johnny was a third-round draft choice and that he could have written his own ticket, but he turned them down."

Now there was a little mystery to figure out, Bailey thought. None of her business, though. Still, she had an irrational craving to know more about Johnny. Considering her attitude toward all other men, she was puzzled by her conflicting emotions.

What was it about Johnny that had made her hormones kick in after an eleven-month vacation? Was it the way he looked so damned sexy in a uniform? It certainly wasn't his laid-back "Let's sleep on it" attitude.

"Why isn't he married?" she asked as casually as possible, so her aunt wouldn't get the mistaken impression she was romantically interested in him.

Cookie laughed. "Marian would love to know the answer to that question too. She keeps pushing him to get married. All her friends have grandchildren. She wants some too."

"Being stubborn about it, is he?"

"Apparently. He's certainly had enough opportunities to make his mother happy. The ladies are as crazy about him now as they were in high school."

"I'll bet they are." Bailey polished off the brownie and washed it down with the last swallow of cola. "Being an attractive fish in a small pond, he no doubt has his pick and choice of all the available women in town."

Cookie chuckled. "Guess he just hasn't found the right fish to settle down with yet. He dates, but never exclusively."

"Of course not. That's the trouble with men in general." Bailey sighed. "Far too many of them don't want to settle for one little fish when they can have the whole school of fish." Or rent them by the hour, she added silently, depressing the heck out of herself.

That drew a full-fledged laugh from her aunt. "Oh, my cynical little Bailey." She wagged a brownie at her. "I do believe you've spent too much time hanging out with perverts and vice cops. Johnny doesn't act like he's interested in owning all the pretty fish in town. He's turned into a fine man. Rock-steady, that's Johnny. Sweet-to-the-bone and charming. Marian told me he was really looking forward to seeing you again."

Cookie noticed the delicate flush that suddenly stained Bailey's cheeks. Intrigued, she would have loved to test the waters and find out just how interested her niece might be in Johnny. He was so good-natured, he would be the perfect husband for her volatile Bailey. And Cookie completely agreed with Marian that those two would make beautiful babies.

However, Cookie wisely kept silent. She knew Bailey far too well. Try pushing her in one direction, and she resisted with every obstinate little bone in her body.

"Johnny is still the biggest flirt in Profitt," Bailey said in an exasperated tone.

"Did he flirt with you today?"

"Does a bear you-know-what in the woods?"

"Did you flirt back?" Cookie asked hopefully.

"No, I did not." Bailey pushed away from the table. "I insisted we maintain a professional relationship."

"I bet that went over like a fart in church. What an ego-crusher!"

"This conversation is getting entirely out of hand." Bailey's tone was stern, but she ruined the effect by grinning. She shook her head as she stood up. "I'm going to take a shower and change."

Cookie smiled fondly as her niece reached for another brownie on her way out. "Dinner's at six o'clock. I invited Harry Baskin to join us. I hope you don't mind."

Bailey paused at the doorway, turning around. "I don't mind." She smiled. "You've been keeping company with Harry for quite a while. Are you going to marry that notorious canine killer?"

"Eventually." Cookie's eyes sparkled with mischief. "But don't tell him that. I'm having too much fun being pursued."

After Bailey left, Cookie remained at the table and worried about her niece. Bailey had always been so stalwart, even at age five, when her mother had died after a year-long battle with cancer.

At the funeral she remembered Bailey standing so quietly and self-contained beside the grave site. Her brothers, Daryl and Ben, had wept silently. But Bailey, like her father, hadn't shed a tear. Like Jack, if she cried, she cried alone.

How Cookie had begged her brother to allow her and Joe to raise Bailey. Jack had refused. He'd never been one to accept help from anyone,

Cookie thought sadly, not even his own sister. Thankfully, he had agreed to send the child to her every summer to learn, as he called it, "the feminine graces."

Over the past few years she had watched fearfully as Bailey had become even more expert at cutting off feelings she didn't want to deal with and denying what was painful. A trait, Cookie acknowledged with a sigh, she had learned from the father she adored.

Yes, Bailey was her father's daughter. Stubborn, full of pride, and wanting to go it alone. They walked the same walk, had the same short temper, and loved being cops. They both wanted to be the best at what they did, regardless of the cost.

Cookie sighed again. More than anything, she wanted Bailey to be happy. Before it was too late, she hoped her niece would come to understand the things Jack never had. Going it alone was just pride disguised as independence. A person could only deny her feelings for so long before those suppressed emotions exploded. Being the best was meaningless if one had to sacrifice everything else in life to achieve it.

Johnny Hart was an indecisive clod. He had no redeeming qualities. He was an idiot for keeping a law officer of her caliber dangling while he pondered needlessly upon a decision that should have been resolved immediately.

So what if he looked good in a uniform? Bailey asked herself. So what if he had a smile that melted her resolve to keep a professional distance? He was a *man*. And men were about as appealing to her as poisonous mushrooms.

Tired of tossing and turning, of listening for the familiar sounds of the city that weren't there, Bailey got out of bed and pulled a robe on over her nightshirt and heavy cotton socks.

Moonlight drifted into the small attic bedroom. She smiled fondly as she glanced around. Aunt Cookie and Uncle Joe, eager to fulfill their longings for a child through their niece, had spared no expense in turning this room with its low, slanted ceiling into a little girl's dream, with picture-perfect white French Provincial furniture, a big canopy bed, pastel prints, and eyelet lace. A Victorian dollhouse stood in one corner.

Tomboy that she'd been at age five, she'd considered the decor too sissy for her, but she'd never said so. Primary colors, plain fabrics, and bunk beds would have thrilled her then. Now she found it all rather sweet and charming. Funny how time altered one's perceptions and attitudes.

"What an ungrateful brat I was." She wandered over to a set of bookshelves filled with stuffed animals, books, and delicate figurines. She smiled as she ran her fingers over a floppy-eared bunny her uncle had helped her win at a county fair.

"They were so good to me." They had given her a beautiful room, love, and affection. To admit she'd been happier there, felt more loved there, felt more at home there, seemed an outrageous transgression against her father and brothers.

Bailey drifted to the window. Her gaze traveled over a huge maple tree. If she opened the window, she could touch one of its thick, snow-covered branches. Uncle Joe had once threatened to chop it down. She grinned. At the time, an eleven-year-old Johnny had been sitting on a topmost branch at two in the morning. Johnny had nearly broken his neck scrambling down. His parents had grounded him for a week.

Beyond the maple tree, separated by two driveways, was the home of the Hart family. Johnny's bedroom had been on the second floor, his window facing hers. For a moment she half expected to see the beam of a flashlight coming from his window, searching for an answering beam of light from hers. Oh, but how illicitly exciting it had been to send secret midnight signals back and forth!

He wasn't there now, she reminded herself. He had a home of his own, built beside a lake on the outskirts of town. So she'd been told.

How simple everything had seemed back then. Bailey sighed as she lifted her hand and pressed it to the cold glass pane.

She and Johnny had had such great fun together as children. They'd been skinny and strong and utterly fearless. Life had been lived for fun.

When had life stopped being fun?

Why couldn't she stop thinking about Johnny Hart?

Bailey didn't have the time to ponder either of those questions. She went on instant alert as a shadow of movement below caught her eye.

A dark figure came around the side of the house and moved across the glistening snow. She assumed from the height and breadth of the dark-clad figure that it was a man. A man with a little breaking and entering on his mind.

She watched him stop and look around. Was he

listening for the warning bark of a dog, watching for any sign of waking and awareness from the two houses?

Then he glanced up toward her window. Bailey dragged in a harsh breath. She could swear he was staring right at her. Instinctively, she swung around, pressing her back to the wall.

Had he seen her?

No, she decided, he couldn't have. She edged around and peered out the window again. He had moved to the base of the maple tree. He stood with one hand on its broad trunk.

Surely he wasn't thinking of climbing it, hoping to find the second-story window unlocked? Good Lord, he was. He swung himself up onto the lowest branch, then onto another.

Bailey checked the window. It was locked. She unlocked it. Might as well make his act of breaking and entering a little easier. No sense in having to replace a busted windowpane.

Calmly, she padded across the room to her overnight bag. Rummaging inside it, she took out a 9-mm automatic pistol and a full clip of ammunition. She slid the clip in at the bottom of the gun handle, shoved it into place, and flicked the safety off.

Scanning the room, she sought out the best vantage point from which to surprise the would-be burglar. The tall chest of drawers at the far end of the room would provide good cover. She moved into position.

And Johnny had said nothing ever happened in Profitt, she thought, smiling smugly. Wait until she served him a second-story man on a silver platter. She was going to enjoy watching the sheriff eat his words!

Time stretched out like a rubber band just waiting to snap back. Tension invaded her muscles. She listened to the whisper of silence broken only by the sound of her own breathing.

Twice she heard a sharp crack. Icicles? Tree branches? A falling burglar?

The room suddenly darkened, and she realized the intruder must have reached the branch closest to the window. His body was blocking the moonlight. Adrenaline shot through her veins like a jolt of electricity.

She heard a soft tapping on the window. Her brow furrowed. An intruder who knocked before entering? Testing the glass? What an idiot.

Silence.

Tapping. Whistling.

Was this guy some kind of psycho?

Blood pounded in her ears. What the hell was the whistling bandit waiting for? An invitation to enter and rob? Maybe she ought to be armed with a straitjacket and butterfly net instead of a gun.

She heard a muffled curse. The tapping started up again. This time she noticed a pattern to it. It was the old "shave and haircut, six bits" routine, followed by the same whistled tune.

She stiffened in complete astonishment. A chaos of emotions and cross signals rampaged through her.

"Unbelievable," she whispered, then silently tacked on a few rude curses. She quickly removed the ammunition clip, dropped it into the pocket of her robe, and flicked the safety on her pistol.

Bailey stalked across the room. Just for the hell

of it, she made sure her weapon was clearly visible to the intruder. He deserved a good scare.

She raised the window. "John Franklin Hart, get your butt in here. You idiot! You're lucky I didn't shoot first and ask questions later."

# *Four*

Johnny's legs were spread wide as he straddled a thick oak branch, one hand planted firmly on another tree limb level with his shoulder. "Hello, Bailey. Did I scare you?" He leaned forward and put his other hand on the window frame. His white teeth flashed in the bright winter moonlight, and she knew Johnny was laughing at her.

"Hell no." She bent over from the waist and rested one elbow on the sill.

"You look pretty in the moonlight." His face was less than twelve inches from hers.

"Don't flirt with me." She raised her other hand and pointed the gun at his nose, and his eyes widened quite satisfactorily. "I thought you were a burglar, and I was just waiting for you to get a leg into the room before I scared the living daylights out of *you*."

"Brat, is that thing loaded?" He pressed his index finger lightly on the barrel, moving the gun away from his face.

She grinned. "That's for me to know and you to find out."

He started. "Oh Lord! I have a feeling I know what your plan was. You thought you'd show up the local yokels by capturing a *burglar* and arrogantly handing him over to me." He tapped her elbow with his finger. "Weren't you?"

"I refuse to answer that question on the grounds that it may incriminate me," she answered loftily.

"I knew it. Move out of the way, brat. I'm coming in."

"Be careful." She straightened and stepped back. "I'd hate it if you fell and broke your foolish neck."

"How sweet of you to worry about my safety," he said cheerfully. "I was beginning to think you didn't care."

*I don't*, she started to say, but it wasn't true. She clamped her lips together and watched the best part of her childhood scramble over the windowsill.

Then Johnny was inside the room and shutting out the cold as he closed the window.

"What are you doing here?"

"I want to ask you a question," he said, "and I want a brutally honest answer. Don't spare my feelings, just tell me what you think from the heart."

"If you want to know if I think you're crazy, then the answer is a definite yes." She crossed her arms and stared hard at him. "I can't believe you pulled such an outrageous, juvenile stunt. You're the sheriff, an officer of the law. Stop grinning at me!"

"You're not playing the game right," he chided.

"Now here's the question. Who is the greatest tree-climber you've ever met? The answer should immediately, reverently spring to your lips."

"Me."

He shook his head. "Wrong. You're second-best. I am and always will be the greatest. Olympic gold material."

A faint smile came to her along with the remembrance of half-forgotten childish banter. "In your dreams, toad face. Your male ego has warped your brain."

"Most women would love having a man scale a tree for them in the middle of the night. It's romantic, don't you know. You ought to be flattered. I haven't climbed a tree in years."

He glanced out the window. "It's trickier than I remembered. Funny, it used to seem so easy. I could do it with one hand tied behind my back and my eyes closed."

"I'm not most women," she responded dryly. "It isn't romantic. It's stupid and dangerous. You're too old for this kind of nonsense."

"It's a good thing I've got a healthy ego," he grumbled. "I'm not that old."

"You're older than you used to be."

"Aren't we all?"

His gaze slowly swept the chamber. "Talk about time warps. Your room still looks the same. Too prissy for a tomboy like you." He grinned, and she worked hard not to be taken in by his charm.

"The room may not have changed, but we have. We're not kids anymore." She frowned and narrowed her eyes. "Do you make a habit of prowling around in the dark and peeking at women through their bedroom windows? That kind of behavior is reprehensible for any adult male and especially reprehensible for an officer of the law."

"Oh, cheer up, Bailey. You're just mad because you didn't get to shoot me." He unzipped his parka and shrugged out of it.

He was wearing jeans and an off-white fisherman's sweater and running shoes. Bailey continued to frown, but it was now directed at herself for appreciating that he looked just as good in casual attire as he did in a uniform.

"Do you sleep with your gun under your pillow?" he asked, abandoning the parka on a chair.

"Of course. It comes in handy when an uninvited guest comes in through the window."

"Am I so unwelcome?" he asked softly.

She found his presence disturbing, but she really couldn't say he was unwelcome. "No, I guess not." Sighing, she turned away to place the gun on the bedside table and switch on a lamp.

"Hey, you still have Myrtle the Turtle!" Johnny said in a loud whisper from the other side of the room.

"What?" She saw him standing in front of the shelves filled with her playthings.

He turned around and held up a fuzzy purple tortoise. His grin was as wide as the one stitched on Myrtle's silly turtle face; as wide and happy as it had been the night he won the prize for her in a ring-toss game at the county fair. They'd been twelve and thirteen.

Bailey smiled, remembering how she'd slept with that stuffed animal all summer. "I'd forgotten about her. I guess Aunt Cookie saved her for me."

He replaced Myrtle on the shelf and glanced

around the room. "We spent hours talking up here, remember?"

"Yes." A lot of hours, both sanctioned and unsanctioned.

Johnny crossed to the canopy bed and dropped down onto it, near the footboard.

Bailey had to smile. He looked so relaxed and so totally out of place lounging on that ultrafeminine piece of furniture. "It feels strange to be here again," she said. "Strange for us to be here together. You remind me of a childhood that seems so distant and far away."

"You remind me of good times and the best friendship I ever had." He flashed her a smile, one sweet enough to melt the heart right out of her body. "We fit together like two pieces in a jigsaw puzzle. We amused each other all the time. That's a very rare thing. I miss having someone like you around."

The girl in Bailey carried the memories of a friendship so deep, so true, she'd never known its equal. A part of her yearned for the kind of close friendship she'd had with Johnny. He had once been very important to her. She doubted if it was possible for them to be that close as adults. But establishing an open line of communication surely couldn't hurt. Could it?

She sat on the bed with her back to the headboard and wrapped her arms around her knees. "We used to have great fun together when we were kids. Remember the gymnastic tricks we used to challenge each other to do? Handstands, back flips, flying somersaults, half gainers off the diving board at the community swimming pool."

"The human-cannonball trick!" Johnny reached

across the bed and snagged a pillow to put under his head. "That one landed you flat on your back and knocked you out cold. I thought you were dead. Scared me so bad, I almost wet my pants."

She laughed. "I was too hardheaded to be really hurt." She leaned forward and rested her chin on her knees. "Comes from being raised with two rough-and-tumble brothers, I guess."

He flipped over onto his side. "That's for sure. Two seconds later you were up and punching me in the stomach for not catching you like I was supposed to. Remember how we used to send secret midnight signals with flashlights back and forth between our houses?"

Bailey laughed again. "I was standing at the window thinking about that just before I saw you skulking around the yard."

"I wasn't skulking." Stretching his arm out, he began to massage the sole of one of her sock-covered feet.

She pushed his hand away with her other foot. "You were definitely skulking."

"No way. Sheriffs do not skulk." He smiled. "Do you want to be friends again?"

"I guess so," she was startled into saying. "You didn't climb a tree in the middle of the night to ask me if I want to be friends again?"

"Sort of," Johnny said, watching her intently. "Do you still believe you want to work for me?"

"Yes." She was silent for an instant. "What happened to *sleeping* on that decision?" Her body stiffened. "If you came here thinking we could sleep on it together, think again," she said, and Johnny heard real hostility in her voice.

"Shame on you, brat. The thought never

crossed my mind." The horrible truth was that it hadn't just crossed his mind, it had taken up permanent residence. "I may have developed an intense physical attraction for your gorgeous body, but I wouldn't act on it unless you issued me an engraved invitation." A smile lifted the corners of his mouth. "You don't happen to have one handy, do you?"

She visibly relaxed. "Forget it, toad face. It ain't gonna happen."

"That's what I thought." He heaved an exaggerated sigh that made her smile. "If you're so determined to work for me, you're hired. Stop by the office before you leave town tomorrow, and we'll work out the necessary details."

"I accept your offer."

"Then it's settled." He sat up and reached over to give her knee a friendly cuff. "A month from now, when you're sitting in the station house on your cute fanny, twiddling your thumbs, just don't come whining to me about how nothing ever happens in Profitt."

Her mouth fell open at the insult. "I've never whined in my life."

"Bitching. You're real good at bitching." He laughed when her foot connected with his ribs. "Watch it, brat. Don't start a war you can't finish."

"Ha! I can still beat you up, toad." Her smile was smug.

"The hell you can. I'm bigger than you are now. Look at this muscle." He flexed one arm. "Like a rock. Go ahead, feel it."

"No way. I don't want your cooties on me. You might have more muscle, but I'm still twice as mean as you." She grinned. "I fight dirty too."

"Amen to that. I almost bled to death that time you broke a cup over my head."

She stared at him. "I never did such a thing."

"Did too. We were playing up at the lake, and all of a sudden you smashed a china cup on my head. Took five stitches to close up the wound."

He crawled up beside her. Bending his head, he raked through his hair at the crown. "There's the scar. See it?"

"I don't see anything." Bailey leaned closer, peering at the top of his head.

"It's there." He took her hand, placing her fingers on his scalp. The warmth of his touch startled her, and she stared at his hand, marveling that it was twice the size of hers. She could feel his strength. His fingers could easily crush hers, she thought. Yes, there was power in his hand, and a gentleness in his touch that took her breath away.

"Feel it?" he asked huskily.

Bailey didn't answer. Her mouth felt dry, and her heart was pounding. He looked up, staring at her with an intensity that made her tremble inside. She jerked her hand away. The abruptness of the action embarrassed her.

"I remember now," she said, all humor gone from her voice. "I was playing near the water with an old chipped cup Aunt Cookie gave me. You came up behind me and put a fish down the back of my shirt."

Johnny continued looking at her, puzzled. Something had shifted within him. Something fast and inevitable. For a moment he'd thought the same thing had happened to her. Then she'd flinched and pulled her hand away as though she'd been burned. Now she sat rigid, looking anywhere and everywhere but at him. He wanted this soft and beautiful woman very much. It shook him to think she might not feel the same as he.

"It was a little fish," he murmured, moving back down to the end of the bed. "Did I do something wrong?"

She laughed, and it sounded forced to him. "No. Of course not."

Johnny had always prided himself on being a sensible man. What he'd done that night didn't even have a nodding acquaintance with good sense. He'd come to see her because he hadn't been able to sleep or think of anything but her. Had he made a mistake by acting so impulsively? he wondered, gazing at her.

Without makeup, her hair artlessly tousled, and her slim body wrapped in a white robe as soft and fleecy as a freshly washed lamb, she seemed girlishly fragile. That fragility was offset by her incorruptible carriage of a lioness and her incredible green eyes, which were capable of hiding her emotions or giving him the Big Chill.

If he were smart, he'd beg her pardon for the intrusion and go home. If he still retained an ounce of sense, he'd ignore the way she put him on full sexual alert and turned his emotions inside out.

With a shake of his head Johnny gave in to the unexplainable feelings that had driven him from his warm bed and out into the frigid night. "Are you seeing anyone in Cleveland?"

Her eyes widened. "No."

"I'm not seeing anyone now either." He rolled onto his back and contemplated the frilly canopy above him. "I was dating Caroline Maxwell. You might remember her. She's Doc Case's daughter. Caro came back home after she got divorced a couple of years ago."

"Pretty girl with lots of blond hair? The homecoming queen?" He nodded. "I remember her. She wouldn't play softball with us because she might break a fingernail. But she would just happen to stroll by in her skimpy little halter top and the tightest shorts in creation, and all the guys would drool over her. You were no exception. I hope she got fat and ugly."

"Sorry. Caro is still blond and beautiful." He grinned at her. "Definite drool material."

Bailey felt her stomach clench up and couldn't for the life of her understand why she gave a rip about Johnny dating Caroline. It had seemed so right just sitting and talking with him—until he had looked at her with undisguised desire and reminded her that he was a man. A man who looked at her with desire in his eyes.

Dismay rippled through her. That emotion was followed by sadness. She had once trusted her old friend Johnny. Would she ever be able to trust the man he had become?

"If she's so blond and beautiful, why did you stop dating her?" she asked, her curiosity getting the better of her.

"She wanted to get married."

"And of course you didn't. How typically male." She scowled, feeling incensed on Caroline's behalf and oddly relieved at the same time.

He gave her a considering look. "It wouldn't have been right."

"Why not?" she demanded. "Too busy playing the field? Too afraid of the C-word?"

Johnny sat up. His gaze remained on her face, searching for a clue to the Big Chill that had once again invaded her eyes. "I've outgrown the playing field, and I'm not afraid of commitment. I couldn't marry Caro because I would have been marrying her for her kids."

"She has children?"

He smiled. "A boy and a girl. Two of the greatest kids I've ever met." His smile faded, and his voice took on a serious tone. "Caro's a nice woman. I like her a lot. It took me a while to realize I enjoyed being with her kids more than I enjoyed being with her. She deserves a man who loves her for herself, not just for her children. Caro wasn't heartbroken when we stopped seeing each other, if that's what's bothering you."

"Why should it bother me?" she asked nonchalantly.

Why indeed? he wondered. "I guess I should go."

He stood up and glanced down at her. Passion seared through him. Kissing her soft, inviting mouth would be heaven. Dammit, she made him feel eighteen and randy again.

Friendship, he told himself. She didn't want to be anything more than friends. Every time he touched her, every time he got a little too close, she seemed not so much to freeze up as to go on guard. He wished he knew the cause of her wariness. In time he hoped she would feel comfortable enough to confide in him.

He smiled and held out his hand. "Come on, friend. Walk me downstairs. I'm too old to leave the way I came in."

"I told you so."

Bailey slipped off the bed and slid her hand into

his. The jolt she received from the physical contact was both thrilling and alarming. What would it be like to kiss that slow, lazy smile right off his face? she wondered. Her grin faded. She yanked her hand free and stepped away from him.

They could be nothing more than friends. The physical attraction would pass, she promised herself. The timing wasn't right. She wasn't comfortable with the idea of allowing herself to become involved in a physical relationship, and hoping for anything else with the biggest flirt in Profitt was unwise.

"Johnny?"

"What?" He looked at her with eyes soft and sensual.

She drew in a quick breath. "I do want the job. But I think it's only fair to tell you . . ." She faltered.

"Tell me what?"

She swallowed. "It's temporary. I'm taking the job for a year at most. I want the experience of small-town law enforcement. Then I'm moving on."

Johnny knew that look, that stubborn tilt of her chin, that tone of her voice. Once she made up her mind about something, she was hardheaded, determined, and impatient. He was determined and *patient* himself.

"All right, Bailey." He kept his voice reassuring and his gaze steady, because she seemed to need it. "I understand. The Sheriff's Department will be fortunate to have you for a year."

"Thank you." The words sounded like a sigh of relief to Johnny.

What in hell had happened to her to make her

act so skittish? he wondered. Was it him? Or was it all men?

Johnny picked up his parka, wondering if 365 days would be long enough for him to find out what made Bailey tick.

*"You asked Bailey to live with you?"* Harry Baskin lost his grip on the deck he was shuffling, and fifty-two cards slithered across the bridge table.

He shifted uncomfortably. The other three members of the Saturday Night Bridge Club were staring at him in unison. Harry wasn't certain which surprised them more, his dramatic outburst or his unusual display of butterfingers.

"Yes, Harry, I did," Cookie answered cheerfully. "I'm tired of rambling around in this big house alone. I can't wait to have her here with me again. I've missed her so much."

Harry looked at Cookie in distress. His beloved wouldn't have to live alone if she'd give in and marry him. "Won't that put a crimp in her social life?" It would sure shoot the hell out of his. "She's young and single. I can't imagine she'd be happy hanging around with us old farts."

"There's plenty of single young men in town," Marian piped up.

"Name one."

"Johnny." Marian turned to Cookie. "Do you remember how Bailey and Johnny used to get into the most ridiculous scrapes? I'll never forget the time those two little dickenses stole Harry's *Playboy* magazines and hid them under Johnny's bed."

Cookie laughed. "Remember the fit old man Porter threw when they climbed up on the roof of his grocery store? Bailey said they were on a 'stakeout' to catch robbers!"

Marian's eyes lit up. "Wouldn't it be something if she and Johnny got together after all these years? Imagine the beautiful babies they'd have."

"A grandchild would be nice," Frank Hart agreed.

Harry threw his brother-in-law a disgusted look. He wondered if the placid smile on Frank's face was caused by the thought of dangling a grandbrat on his knee or by the bowl of potato chips Frank had his eye on. He'd bet on the chips. Frank was addicted to junk food. Marian was addicted to keeping her husband on her saltless, sugarless diet.

"Maybe Johnny isn't ready to settle down and supply you with grandbabies," Harry said to his sister.

"Of course he's ready to settle down." Marian launched into a rhapsody about the prospect of marrying her darling boy off to Cookie's niece.

Harry listened with growing dismay. He wanted to give his sister's ankle a swift kick under the table the way he used to do when they were kids. She knew darn well he was trying to convince Cookie to marry him and move to Florida! Hell's bells, if Marian got a bee in her bonnet over this matchmaking thing, he knew he could kiss his own plans good-bye.

"Must we talk about the brats?" he said. "I'd like to finish this rubber before I die of old age." Harry rapidly shuffled the cards. The only marital state he was interested in was his own. Sixty-five years was long enough to be single.

Cookie gave him an indulgent smile. "Now, Harry, your nephew and my niece are too old to be called brats." She went back to the discussion at hand.

Harry seethed silently. It had taken him four years to convince Cookie to officially keep company with him, after her husband died. He was having a hell of a time persuading her to marry him, because he wanted to leave Profitt. If he had to spend one more winter knee-deep in snow—

A shriek startled Harry as he dealt out the last card.

"Don't you dare eat that potato chip, Franklin Hart!" Marian gave her husband "the look" she'd perfected from years of teaching English to thick-headed high school students.

"Aw, nuts." Frank dropped the forbidden chip.

"Have a carrot stick," his wife ordered. "Now how are we going to get Johnny and Bailey together?"

"They *are* adults," Harry said. "Let 'em worry about their own damn affairs."

"I love Bailey like she was my own." Cookie gathered up her cards. "I want her to be happy." She shot a veiled look at Harry. "If I knew she was settled and happy, I just might consider moving to Florida with a certain gentleman."

Harry knew he was fighting a losing battle. He gave up his objections with a sigh. If his beloved wanted to hitch her niece to his nephew, so be it. He'd move heaven and earth to help her achieve her heart's desire. Anything that got them both on the road to the land of sunshine was fine by him.

On that bright note he sorted his cards and opened the bidding with one spade.

# Five

One hour into her first day on the job Bailey decided it was only a matter of time before she shot the sheriff.

The day had begun well enough with the morning shift meeting. She met the officers going off duty and the ones coming on duty, and was pleased to discover she was one of four females in the department. Not a bad ratio, considering the size of the staff. Everyone was friendly, and they made her feel welcome.

Johnny impressed her with the way he easily assumed command of the meeting. He listened to reports from the officers going off duty and ensured that all paperwork and unserved warrants were reassigned to officers coming on duty. He assigned cases and made decisions on how to handle ongoing investigations.

Johnny might talk slow, walk slow, and look indolent, but she knew that was all deceptive. The man was sharp, and he ran a tight ship. It was obvious he respected his staff and they respected him. Bailey couldn't help feeling something very close to pride over the aura of strength, calmness, and competency he projected.

Things took a downhill slide at the end of the meeting, when Johnny turned to his administrative assistant and said, "Make sure you order Detective Asher's uniforms today."

"Uniforms?" Bailey blurted out. She hadn't worn them since her rookie days, and damned if she'd wear one now. "I thought I could wear plain clothes."

"A uniform would be more appropriate," Johnny answered, smiling. "Makes you more visible and easily identifiable in the community."

"But I'd prefer plain clothes."

"I'd prefer that you didn't." He'd lost the smile.

Bailey launched into all the reasons why she shouldn't be required to wear a uniform. She noticed that the rest of the staff listened with avid interest, their glances swinging from her to the sheriff and back again.

"You will be in uniform," Johnny ordered when she finally fell silent.

His gentle tone of voice didn't fool Bailey for an instant. She had lost. To continue arguing was useless.

"You have three days' grace," he told her generously, "the time it will take to order the garments. Okay, folks, if that's it. Let's get to work."

Everyone stood up.

"Sheriff Hart, just one more thing," Bailey called out.

Everyone sat down again and looked at her as though waiting to see what bomb she'd drop next.

"I'd like to ride along with one of the road deputies today."

There was a long silence, then a long-jawed, barrel-chested deputy scratched his chin and said, "I don't mind if she rides with me."

Bailey smiled. "Thank you, Deputy Adkins."

Johnny turned to glare at the officer. "You may not mind, but I do. Everyone is dismissed. Please stay for a minute, Detective Asher."

Bailey felt her face turning pink.

After bouncing a few grins and curious glances at their sheriff and their embarrassed new colleague, the rest of the staff filed out.

Johnny stared at her. She matched him frown for frown, then spoke first. "What's the problem? I thought I made a perfectly good suggestion."

"It wasn't a suggestion." He took a few steps toward her. "Are you pricking my temper on purpose?"

"No." As a matter of fact, she had forgotten he had one. "I simply thought riding with one of the road deputies would be a good way to familiarize myself with the county." She hid her exasperation. "Jumping right into fieldwork would give me a better idea of the kind of routine calls the department handles."

"You've got to learn to walk before you jump, Bailey. You will remain at the station house today to learn the ropes. Familiarize yourself with the policies-and-procedures manual I put on your desk. Go over the old and new files." The glint in his eyes as well as the hand he held up stopped the complaint forming on her lips.

He left the room. Bailey had no choice but to shut up and follow.

Minutes later, their third disagreement started in the corridor outside Johnny's office.

"Are you serious?" she asked incredulously, frowning down at the sheet of paper he had just handed her. "This is a joke, right?" She looked up and smiled, showing her willingness to be a good sport.

"It isn't a joke," he said, acting as though there was nothing unusual about his request as he leaned against the wall. "These people look forward to their morning calls. They live alone, and they are elderly. If they get sick or fall, they can stay there for days and no one will know."

Bailey didn't try to hide her exasperation. Her hands settled on her hips. "Surely there's some agency or social organization that could provide this service? This kind of thing takes up valuable time. In the city—"

"Bailey, I don't give a damn how things are done in the big city."

"I don't believe this." She released an exaggerated sigh.

Johnny gazed at her through half-shuttered eyes. He had always considered himself a patient man. Bailey was sorely testing that image of himself. He wondered how he was going to survive her first day on the job without either kissing her or wrapping his hands around her throat.

"You and I are going to come to an understanding," he told her in a no-nonsense tone of voice. "I'm the sheriff. You work for me. That means I'm the chief and you're the Indian. I give the orders and you carry them out. No insubordination tolerated."

Her eyes flashed. "I'm not trying to be insubordinate."

He folded his arms and stared hard at her. Even with a pouty expression on her face, she looked damned pretty. "Sounds like insubordination to me."

"Well, it isn't."

He said nothing, but couldn't help smiling a little. He liked the way her snippy little nose went up in the air and her eyes sparkled when she was mad. He doubted Bailey had ever toed the line with anyone. It would be too much of a strain for her to meekly obey without getting her two cents' worth in first.

"I'm merely trying to point out to you," she went on, "that my time could be better utilized investigating crimes than chatting with shut-ins."

He let out a sigh. "A half hour or so, Bailey, that's all it will take of your *valuable* time." His voice grew serious. "We've been calling the elderly and the sick for eight months. It's worked very well so far. The elderly deserve a little special consideration. They've made their contributions to this community, and it's only right that the community give something back."

"I agree. But—"

"Fine," he said curtly. "Go make your calls." He couldn't afford to let her get the upper hand. He had to establish his authority immediately or she would think she could walk all over him and do as she damn well pleased.

"If someone doesn't answer," he added, "phone their contact person on the list. If the contact person isn't home, let the dispatcher know. She'll send an officer to investigate."

Bailey opened her mouth to continue the argument, but before she got out the first word, he cut her off again. "Just think how you'd feel if your aunt was sick and alone and no one cared enough to make sure she was all right. Wouldn't *you* want someone to check on her?"

That shut her up. The bluster went out of her opposition. Of all the reasons he could have given her, he'd hit on the one she couldn't argue with. But just so he wouldn't think she was a pushover, she gave him a mutinous glare.

Looking as though he wanted to throttle her, he muttered something about her driving him to take up smoking again. He abruptly turned away and went into his office, slamming the door.

"Detective Asher?"

Bailey whirled around to see a young man standing behind her. "Deputy Evans," she said coolly.

"Don't worry, the sheriff won't stay mad at you. He's just touchy about his pet project. Calling the elderly, I mean." The deputy reddened with embarrassment to the roots of his sandy crew cut. "I didn't mean to eavesdrop when you were talking to him. I just wanted to say it's an honor to have a *real* detective like you on staff." His tone of voice bordered on reverence, making Bailey feel uncomfortably like a minor celebrity. "You can call me Tim if you want to. If you need anything, I'll be glad to help you. I'm in the Records Department just down the hall."

Up close, Bailey could see he was only a few years beyond being considered a boy. She bet his parents still called him "Timmy." No doubt he was the most virgin officer on staff, accounting for his

Records assignment. Having been stuck with that job in her rookie days, she sympathized with him. She softened her coolness with a friendly smile. "I appreciate the offer."

"Well, you have a nice day." A smile stretched across his thin face as he backed away. He bumped into the wall and turned bright red. "See you later," he mumbled, and practically fled down the hallway.

Shaking her head in amusement, Bailey headed for her office. The new Investigative Unit was located in an alcove at the end of the corridor. It was right across from a dismal-looking holding cell, which was not occupied at the moment.

She didn't stop to appreciate the new sign on the door with her name and rank. She went inside. For the heck of it she slammed her door and mentally thumbed her nose at the absent Johnny.

Johnny wasn't in a good mood. One fiery, red-headed detective was driving him to distraction in more ways than one. Her gung-ho, big-city attitude was all wrong for Profitt. Her sassy, kissable mouth was going to get her in big trouble. And he wanted to be the trouble she got into.

If Bailey had been prone to claustrophobia, her office would have given her a screaming fit. It was about the size of a supply closet. In fact, she thought, glancing at the wooden shelves along one wall, it probably had been a supply closet until it

had been cleaned out to create the so-called Investigative Unit.

"Depressing" was the best description she could
come up with. A fluorescent ceiling fixture shed
an unkind light on the dull gray linoleum floor
and the walls that badly needed painting. The
office was furnished with a desk, a swivel chair, a
filing cabinet, another chair, and a telephone.
Someone, in an attempt to brighten up the place,
had tacked a floral calendar to one wall and set on
the desk a water glass filled with perky daisies.

Feeling something very close to a sulk coming
on, Bailey flopped down into the swivel chair and
tossed the sheet of paper onto the desk. As she
picked up the phone and dialed the first number
on her list, she decided that Johnny, for all his
easygoing ways, wasn't as persuadable as he had
been when they were kids. He'd grown a large,
unreasonable stubborn streak.

The sheriff also had some strange ideas about
law enforcement. Surely there was something
more productive she could be doing than making
calls to the elderly, for heaven's sake! What would
Johnny order her to do next? Teach the prisoners
to knit?

She drummed her nails on the desk, counting
the number of rings. How long was she supposed
to wait for an answer? When the phone had rung
at least twenty times, she couldn't help becoming
concerned.

Finally, a thin, wavering voice came on the line,
saying hello.

Bailey breathed a sigh of relief and introduced
herself. "How are you, Mrs. Sheldon?"

"Just fine, thank you. It's so nice of you ask. I do

so look forward to my morning call. It's one of the nicest things that has ever happened in this town. Tell me, dear, what kind of day is it outside today?"

At that moment Bailey's heart went into the task she had considered a waste of law-enforcement time. "It's very cold. The air is crisp and clean, and it smells like snow. The sky is blue-gray with clouds. . . ."

Forty minutes later she had made all the calls on her list and slumped back in her chair. Her face burned with shame, and she was glad no one was around to witness it. Swallowing hard, she opened her eyes wide and stared at the ceiling. It was a trick she'd learned a long time ago to prevent the fall of tears.

There was a knock on the door. She hastily pulled herself together and sat up straight. "Come in."

Johnny entered. He held out a cup of coffee. "You can have this if you promise not to throw it at me."

"As tempting as that sounds, I believe I need the caffeine more." She smiled her thanks as he handed her the steaming beverage. "How did you know I like it black?"

"I asked your aunt. Mrs. Hoover said you like it black, hot, and strong." He sat down, dwarfing the wooden chair.

"Wouldn't it have been easier to ask me?" She wrapped both hands around the cup and took a sip.

"Yeah. But I wasn't sure if you were speaking to me. You were a bit miffed when we parted a little while ago." He grinned. "Still miffed?"

"No." She tried not to notice how outrageously attractive he was. "You're a thoughtful man."

Johnny's eyes widened. Was she being flippant with him? No, he didn't think so. "I'm sorry about the office. We're a bit short on space and low on funding. This is the best we can do for now."

"It's not so bad."

He grinned. "That's a crock."

She grinned back. "Okay, it's the pits, but it can be fixed. Can the department afford a gallon of paint?"

"I think the budget can stand the cost."

She gestured toward the daisies. "Who do I thank for the flowers?"

"Consider it an office-warming present from the staff," he said, not wanting to risk her disapproval by admitting he was solely responsible. "Have you finished making your calls?"

She nodded and took another sip of coffee. "Apologizing isn't easy for me. But in all fairness, I owe you one."

His brows shot upward. "Is that so?"

She spoke in a rush, the words tumbling out one after another. "I'm sorry for making such a fuss about checking on the elderly. I honestly wasn't trying to be insubordinate. In the city our caseloads are so heavy, we would never have time for that kind of public service. I guess we become so caught up in the protecting part of our job that we forget we're also there to serve." She lowered her gaze. "I was . . . was wrong to imply it was a waste of time."

She looked so uncomfortable with her confession, Johnny wanted to hug her. Instead, he reached out and captured one of her hands. Surprise flared in her eyes, but she didn't pull away. "It's okay, Bailey. You just have to remember that small towns are like family. We look out for one another. The people elected me as sheriff because they knew I'd look out for their interests as well as uphold the law. Sometimes it's more important to exercise the spirit of the law instead of the letter of the law. Know what I mean?"

She lightly squeezed his fingers. "You have a caring nature."

"How would you know what's in my nature?" he asked, curious to hear what she would say.

"I know the daily check on the elderly was your idea. Deputy Evans told me it was your pet project." She waved her hand toward the glass of flowers. "I know you put those daisies on my desk, even though you denied it. And there are dozens of examples I could give you from when we were kids."

"Hell, you make me sound like a pretty fine fellow."

"Well, you have a few good qualities in spite of the fact that you're a man."

He caught the words "in spite of" and "man," but decided against questioning her. Though she'd spoken lightly, he suspected his instincts were right. Bailey definitely had some kind of problem with men.

"So did you enjoy talking to the people on your list?" he asked, deliberately changing the subject.

"I did enjoy it, but it was sad too. Everyone I talked to was so grateful, it made my heart ache. Some of them sounded so lonely, I felt guilty for keeping the conversations short." She averted her gaze for a second, then looked back at him, smiling. "Mr. Parker told me his joke of the day. Want to hear it?"

"Sure."

"A doctor walks into a patient's room and says, 'I have good news. A team of physicians think you're strong enough to see your bill.'"

Johnny grinned and shook his head. "Mr. Parker spends a lot of time at the hospital. Heart problems. He's got a million doctor jokes."

"Do I contact the same people every morning?"

"Yes. It means a lot to them to hear a familiar voice." He rubbed his thumb over her knuckles, and Bailey thought how nice it felt having him hold her hand. "Not only is it a pleasant way to start their day, it makes us feel good too."

She nodded. It certainly beat standing on street corners busting petty criminals. "One woman asked me to tell her what kind of day it was outside. A Mrs. Sheldon. Is she blind?" In a minute she would politely remove her hand from his. But not yet.

"No. She's eighty, though, and her eyesight is failing." He slowly worked his way from one knuckle to another. Her skin felt better than satin. "Mrs. Sheldon is a doll. I'll take you to meet her sometime. She taught high school science for more years than anyone can remember. Would you have dinner with me tonight?"

Her answer was to give him one of those damn skittish looks as she snatched her hand from his.

"I think you should," he persisted.

"Why?"

"Because we're friends." There were other reasons, but he'd keep them to himself for now. "We've got a lot of lost years to catch up on."

"I don't know," she hedged. "This is my first day at work. I'm just getting settled in at Aunt Cookie's house."

"Look, I'll be at the Market Street Café at seven. If you can make it, great. If not I'll catch you another time." He gazed at her, completely guileless. "Of course, it will break my heart if I have to eat alone."

After a long moment she smiled. "You are incorrigible."

"Is that what I am?"

"Among other things."

"You're probably right." He had to quit staring at her, and the only way he could do that was to leave. If she knew how powerless he was against this attraction, she'd probably die. Or kill him. He stood and walked to the door. There, he turned and casually asked, "Will I see you at dinner?"

She hesitated. "I suppose the café has a deluxe dinner special?"

"Spaghetti. All you can eat for four ninety-five."

Bailey realized she had just agreed to meet him for dinner and let out a little sigh. "May I ride with one of the deputies tomorrow to familiarize myself with the county and the day-to-day routine calls?"

"Let me sleep on that."

She groaned and half covered her face with her hand. "The last time you said that, you crawled through my window in the middle of the night. I'm warning you, stay out of my tree and out of my room."

He just grinned and opened the door. "Try to stay out of trouble," he said on his way out.

Bailey sat there feeling light-headed, off balance. In an effort to restore her calm, she took a deep breath, then released it slowly. One dinner with a friend didn't mean anything. It would be fun. They could talk about old times and do a little shop talking, buddy-to-buddy. Nothing to it, right?

Wrong. It would be sheer hell.

Johnny would flirt because flirting came as naturally to him as breathing. She'd make a fool of herself by overreacting to it whether she meant to or not.

He would touch her because he was a toucher. He came from a family of unconscious touchers and huggers. And heaven help her, she'd probably react badly to that too.

She had a horrible feeling that before they could eat all the spaghetti they wanted for $4.95, Johnny would think she was frigid or schizophrenic. Not a pretty picture.

Oh come on, she chided herself. It was ridiculous to think a simple dinner between friends would turn into a man-woman thing. "Johnny *is* a friend," she said aloud. It sounded so good, she said it twice more.

Bailey reached for the policies-and-procedures manual lying on the desk. Whoever claimed that whatever was said aloud three times must be true was a flaming idiot.

No way was she going anywhere near the Marker Street Café and Johnny that night.


"Hey! Can anybody hear me?" Bailey shouted again. She wrapped her hands around the holding cell bars and tried shaking them. They wouldn't budge, of course. Now she knew why jailbirds in the movies beat the hell out of their bars with a tin cup. It took the edge off the frustration boiling up inside them. She wished she had a tin cup. Boy, would she make those damn bars sing!

She took two steps to the left and stood directly in front of the security camera on the wall outside the holding cell. Hands on her hips, she glared at it. She damn well knew Deputy Bea Early, the dispatcher on duty, could see her on the monitor. Although Bea couldn't leave the communications area unmanned, she should have sent someone to let Bailey out by now.

Hands still firmly locked on her hips, she began to pace. Of all the stupid predicaments to get herself into. The big-shot Cleveland detective getting locked in a cell! Oh Lord, the jokes she'd have to endure. She'd be the laughingstock of the entire staff for weeks. Worse, the story would be retold at every dinner table all over town.

Storming over to the bunk built into the wall, Bailey flopped down. She glanced at her watch. It was a quarter after twelve. Either everyone was out on call or out to lunch. Unless Bea Early had a sick sense of humor and found her circumstances amusing, those were the only reasons Bailey could think of to explain why no one had come to set her free in the past ten minutes.

She folded her arms over her chest, crossed her legs, and angrily swung her foot to and fro. This wouldn't have happened if Johnny had given her something active to do. It wouldn't have happened if she hadn't been bored to death reading bylaws, policies and procedures, and case files until her eyes crossed.

After three hours of being cooped up in her

windowless, airless office, feeling as if she could climb the walls that were closing in on her, she had gone searching for something to do. Mistake number *one.*

*Big* mistake number two had occurred when she had noticed the unmade bunk in the holding cell. Since the door had been ajar, she'd gone in to tidy up. Bailey blew out a furious breath, ruffling her bangs. Who could have known the cell door would automatically shut behind her?

Hearing the faint but steady sound of footsteps in the corridor, she jumped to her feet. Throwing herself against the steel bars, she started yelling.

Harry Baskin came strolling around the corner. He was tall and slim, handsome in a Douglas Fairbanks, Jr., kind of way. His thick white hair was neatly combed back from a widow's peak. He had an unlit cigar in his mouth and wore perfectly creased trousers and a sports coat. He had the air of the successful attorney he had once been. Bailey knew his crisp white shirt carried his initials on the breast pocket and that his mind was as cunning as any criminal's she'd ever met.

"Hello, girlie," he said around the cigar. "Bea told me you'd gone and got yourself locked up. Just had to come back here and see for myself." He took the cigar out of his mouth and grinned. "Yup, you're locked up tight all right. How'd you get yourself in such a mess?"

"Very funny, Mr. Baskin. Would you please ask one of the deputies to let me out?"

"Everybody's out to lunch except you and Bea, and you know she can't leave the phones untended. Yes sir, I'd say you got yourself into a pickle, girlie." The amusement in Harry's eyes culminated in a big, booming fit of laughter.

Holding on to the ragged edges of her temper, she said sweetly, "Would you please ask Deputy Early to give *you* the key to unlock this cell?"

Harry rocked back on his heels. "Well now, I could do that. Then again, how do I know Johnny didn't throw you in there himself?"

"He didn't. It was an accident."

"I've heard that story before," he said, wagging the cigar at her. "No, I don't think I should take the responsibility of setting you free."

"Mr. Baskin! I realize you find my situation humorous, but—"

"Funniest thing I've seen since the look on Judge Wilkins's face when I convinced a jury that the ten VCRs found in the trunk of my client's car were Christmas gifts from his loving family and friends."

Bailey sighed. "A joke is a joke, but this one has ceased to be amusing. Either get the key and unlock this door or have Bea contact the sheriff."

Harry shook his head. "No can do. Johnny's having lunch with the mayor. So I guess you better get used to the view from where you're standing. Be right back."

"Mr. Baskin?" Seething with anger and frustration, she chewed on her lower lip as she watched him go into her office.

He immediately returned with the wooden chair, which he set in front of the cell. "Slide that table and chair over to the bars, girlie."

"Whatever for?"

Harry pulled a deck of cards out of his pocket. His brown eyes were twinkling. "Girlie, I recognize a captive card player when I see one. Do you know how to play honeymoon bridge?"

"No."

"Poker?"

"Yes, but I'm not playing cards with you."

"You don't have anything better to do. Might as well make good use of your time, girlie. Five-card stud okay with you?"

"Mr. Baskin," she began, then sighed. "Sit down."

Thirty minutes later Bailey had just decided "card sharp" fit Harry as well as "canine killer" and "con man," when she heard footsteps in the corridor. Relief battled with renewed embarrassment as she prayed it was someone coming to set her free.

Johnny came around the corner, his leisurely pace suggesting he was in no hurry at all. She could have kissed him for the key in his hand and punched him for the grin on his face.

His laughing gaze slowly traveled over her, then he peered over his uncle's shoulder at the cards he held. "That's a sorry-looking hand. I'd fold." He glanced back at Bailey and shook his head. "I should have known you couldn't stay out of trouble."

"I didn't go looking for trouble," she said, trying to sound extremely casual. "It was an accident." She tossed her cards down.

"An accident." Johnny's eyes sparkled with amusement.

"Yes, an accident." Lord, he was a handsome devil, she thought. She shook her head, annoyed she'd noticed that despite embarrassment. She knew she was blushing scarlet too. Extreme embarrassment and an insane sexual attraction didn't make good bedfellows.

Johnny chuckled. "'An accident.'" That's what Barney Fife used to tell Sheriff Taylor. Maybe I ought to make you keep a single bullet for your gun in your pocket." His voice took on a kindly tone. "For your own safety, of course. Can't have you accidentally shooting yourself in the foot."

One thing Bailey hated more than apologizing was appearing foolish. She rose and pushed back the chair. "Just unlock the damn cell."

"She seems kinda mad, boy." Harry started gathering up the cards. "Maybe you ought to let her cool off a bit before you let her out. Looks like she could do you some bodily harm." He winked at his nephew.

"*Harry*," she said menacingly. She'd begun calling him by his first name at his insistence. "You can stuff those cards where the sun don't shine."

Both Harry and Johnny burst into laughter.

"If you two are finished laughing and making fun of me, I'd like to get out of here," she said once they'd controlled themselves.

Johnny put the key in the lock. "We weren't laughing at you, *Barney*. We were just teasing a bit, that's all." The cell door swung open.

"In case you didn't notice, I wasn't laughing." She brushed past him, walked stiffly into her office, and slammed the door.

Johnny sighed. "Isn't she cute?"

"Sure is." Harry slanted a sideways glance at his nephew. Never had he seen such a goofy expression on the boy's face. Cookie and Marian weren't going to have any trouble convincing Johnny to be interested in that little girlie.

"Don't you just love the way her nose wrinkles up and her eyes flash like emerald fire when she's mad?"

Harry's brows shot up toward his widow's peak. Beneath his brash exterior beat a kind heart, a heart that recognized another caught in the love trap. The boy was good and hooked. "She's a hellcat, though," he felt obliged to point out.

Johnny grinned. "I noticed."

"A man would have his hands full trying to tame that one."

"Who would be fool enough to want to tame all that fire?" Johnny asked incredulously. "Life with a woman like that would never be dull."

A minute passed with Harry looking at his nephew and his nephew staring at the closed office door as though he could see through it to the object of his affection. "Let me know," Harry said.

"Let you know what?"

"When the wedding's going to be."

"What wedding?" Johnny cast a startled glance at his uncle.

Harry just laughed and walked away. The seed had been planted in the boy's mind, and it would be interesting to see how it grew. He hoped it grew fast. Maybe Cookie would consider having a double wedding with the kids.

He stuck the unlit cigar back into his mouth and started daydreaming about a honeymoon. Would Cookie like a trip to someplace tropical? St. Thomas. Cancun, Mexico. Palm trees and sand, mariachi players, breathtaking sunsets. Warm, lazy days, passionate nights . . .

# *Six*

It wasn't a date. At least, that's what Bailey had told Cookie and Harry on her way out to meet Johnny at the Market Street Café. She couldn't blame them for not believing her, because she didn't believe it herself.

She stood on the sidewalk in front of the café, ten minutes late. It was colder than a witch's cackle, yet she made no move to go inside the warm, brightly lit restaurant.

It's absurd to feel so nervous, she told herself. A thirty-year-old woman ought to be able to keep a simple dinner date with a friend without going bonkers.

Several couples on their way into the café glanced at her questioningly and smiled as if to say, "Aren't you going inside?"

In truth, she wanted as badly to go in as she wanted to turn around and go home. Given the way Johnny made mush of her emotions, spending an evening with him wasn't very prudent.

Yet she couldn't go home.

Cookie was entertaining Harry with a cozy candlelight dinner for two. Bailey didn't want to intrude on their private time, especially if that private time included . . . intimacy.

She didn't know for a fact that sex was a part of their relationship, because she hadn't been able to summon the nerve to ask Cookie. Anyone could see how deeply in love they were, though. Bailey wasn't too keen on that kind of intimacy for herself, but she wasn't prudish enough to begrudge others the need.

Gathering her courage, she marched over to the café entrance. She told herself she was making things harder than they had to be. It was time she started dating again. Tonight could be considered a trial run.

Pushing open the door, she went inside. The café was just as she remembered. Thirteen years had done little to change the atmosphere, which was a curious blend of classic diner fixtures and the homespun decor of Grandma's country kitchen. She nervously finger-combed her bangs back as she looked over the crowd.

She spotted Johnny in a booth near the back. He had company. Female company.

Her heart skipped a beat. Blood drained from her face. She got the same sick feeling in the pit of her stomach that hit her every time she had to bust a married man for solicitation.

Standing still for a moment, she willed herself to be calm and think rationally. Johnny didn't belong to her. He wasn't her husband. He wasn't even her . . . man. A friend, that's all he was. She did not have the right to feel possessive and betrayed. Even so, it hurt more than it should to think he had given up on her so soon, that he had found someone else to flirt with over the deluxe dinner special.

She unclenched her stiff, cold fingers and let out the breath she'd held suspended in her throat. Only an idiot would have fallen for Johnny's "It will break my heart if I have to eat alone" line. He probably had dinner with a different woman every night!

Color returned to Bailey's cheeks in the form of angry splotches. She was on the verge of turning around and walking out when he glanced up and saw her.

He quickly got up and stood beside the booth. Like herself, he'd traded his work clothes for jeans and a sweater—his was red. Apparently, she thought, the devil didn't mind showing his true color. His gaze locked with hers, and a slow, heart-twisting smile formed on his lips.

Forcing an answering smile, she wove through the sea of tables and diners. By the time she reached him, she had decided not to let him matter to her. Still, she had no desire to become a part of his dinner harem for the evening. She'd visit with him and his—his friend for a few minutes, then she would leave.

"Bailey." He infused enough warmth into her name to light a campfire.

"Hello, Johnny," she answered, frowning. She refused to allow his smile to get under her skin and goose her silly hormones.

His smile dissolved. "Is something wrong?" He lifted his hand to stroke her cold cheek.

"What could be wrong?" She turned her head,

and he dropped his hand back to his side. "Everything is just fine." She glanced back at him, her eyes bright with false cheer.

"Okay." He looked unconvinced. "I'm glad you're here. I was beginning to worry you weren't going to make it tonight."

"Were you now?" Bailey glanced at his companion. She was young, cradle-robbing young. Eighteen and trying to look older with enough eye makeup to do all the teenage girls in Profitt. Did the man have no shame? No scruples? No taste?

"I can't stay." Bailey swiveled her head around, giving him a glare that should have burned a hole through his forehead. "I just stopped by to say hello. I can see that you're . . . busy. I don't want to intrude, so I'll just run along." There, now she could leave.

"You're not intruding. We have a date." He clamped a hand around her arm.

"No, we don't. Well, not really."

"Yes. A date."

She felt rather than heard the steely determination in his voice. He was so quick, she found herself hustled into the booth and seated before she had time to object.

Then he was scooting in next to her, and she was trapped between the wall and his body. He smiled at her, and she knew he was well aware of her reluctance to be where she was.

While she debated the consequences of stabbing him in the ribs with a fork, he introduced her to the girl sitting opposite them. Bailey made an appropriate response. She decided the pleasure of forking him wasn't worth going to jail for.

"Heather has a problem," he told Bailey solemnly.

"Really?" She made him the victim of a mocking glance. In her opinion a thirty-one-year-old man fooling around with a teenage girl was a definite problem.

"She wants the Sheriff's Department to help her retrieve some personal property." He picked up a glass of water and took a long swallow, all the while giving Bailey an amused look. "The property in question is one double mattress, box spring, frame, and headboard."

"Oh, I see." Bailey avoided his gaze. She had been right to worry about making a fool of herself that night. Where Johnny was concerned, she was much too good at jumping to the wrong conclusions.

"Explain the problem to Detective Asher, Heather."

Heather eagerly continued her story as Bailey removed her coat. "It's so *AWFUL!*" Heather flopped back against the padded booth and sighed dramatically. "Aunt Ruby is just being plain *MEAN*. It's *MY* bed."

Heather, Bailey noticed right off, exhibited a distressing tendency to sprinkle her speech with words wailed in neon capitals.

"I've got a *RIGHT* to move out and live on my own if I want to. Don't I, Sheriff Hart?" Indignant tears filled her eyes and threatened her Tammy-Faye-Bakker makeup. "I'm *EIGHTEEN*, and I've got a steady job over at the grocery store." She stopped to sniffle.

Johnny stretched across Bailey to pluck a napkin from the dispenser, bringing his torso closer to hers, pressing his thigh against hers. They both froze.

Their gazes locked. Her senses went on alert a heartbeat after his. Pulses quickened. The art of breathing was forgotten. It was a brief instant so purely sensual, everything around them ceased to exist.

Bailey recovered first, drawing back as far as she could. The breath she hadn't been aware of holding came out slowly.

Johnny blinked away the sensuous flame burning in his eyes. Straightening, he handed the napkin to the sniffling girl.

Heather blew her nose loudly. "Aunt Ruby went and changed all the locks on the doors. She won't let me in the house, and she hangs up *EVERY* time I call. I told her I was going to call the *SHERIFF* on her. She said she didn't *CARE,* because possession is nine tenths of the law." There was a pause both in speech and waterworks. "What's the other tenth?"

"The other tenth?" Bailey repeated, smiling to herself. She traded a glance with Johnny. A devilish grin crossed his face and wound up as a twinkle in his eyes.

"I believe Detective Asher can explain the, uh . . . other tenth." He nudged her thigh, and his twinkle brightened.

It took Bailey a moment to answer because Johnny had stretched an arm along the back of the booth and his fingers were playing with her hair. "Your alleged ownership of the bed, Heather," she finally managed to say.

"*ALLEGED?*" The girl's expression clearly stated she didn't know what the word meant, but she was certain it wasn't something she should be happy about. "Is that like saying I'm *LYING*?"

"We're not questioning your integrity," Johnny said soothingly. "It just means you claim the property belongs to you."

"Darn right it does," she yelped. "My *DADDY* gave me that bed. Bought and paid for it before he *RAN* off and *LEFT* me with Aunt Ruby. How *DO* I get my property back?"

Johnny smiled and spoke in a kind tone. "Your aunt is obviously upset about you moving out of her home. She's taken care of you for a long time, and she probably still thinks of you as a little girl. Give her some time to adjust to the realization that you've grown up."

Wanting to be helpful, Bailey added, "If she continues to refuse to give you the bed, you do have the option of settling the matter in small-claims court."

"*SUE* her?"

Johnny saw that Heather was immensely attracted to the notion, because she cheered up enough to beam a sunny smile. He tickled Bailey's sensitive nape and felt her shiver. Smiling, he bent his head and murmured close to her ear, "Way to go. Encourage litigation among Profitt's youth."

He looked at the girl and knew he had to stop her from turning the situation with her aunt into a bigger problem. "You do have the right to take this matter before a judge in small-claims court. However, I advise you to think it over very carefully before you do something that drastic.

"If you wish, Detective Asher and I would be happy to speak to your aunt on your behalf." He smiled and added, "I'm certain an intelligent, mature young woman like yourself would prefer to resolve the issue without going to court."

Good advice, Bailey thought, switching her gaze from Johnny to the teenager. She saw that Heather was not immune to the sheriff's charming smile or his flattery.

"I guess it'd be kinda *TACKY* to sue my own aunt. Miss Asher, Sheriff, thank you *SO* much for letting me talk to you like this. I feel much better knowing you'll *DO* something about this awful *MESS*." She scooted out of the booth, leaving the damp, wadded-up napkin behind.

"Does this sort of thing happen to you often?" Bailey asked, after the girl rejoined her friends at another table.

"Yes. Get used to it. Once people know who you are, you'll probably be subjected to lots of strange requests when you least expect it. In fact, I have one right now. Don't encourage litigation."

She bristled because she thought he was criticizing her for trying to help. "Is that an order, Sheriff Hart?"

He shook his head. "It's a request."

"You don't believe everyone should know what their legal rights are?"

"Of course I believe everyone should know," he said, sounding a little frustrated. "That's not the real issue here. I expect my officers to use a little common sense and try to resolve problems."

Bailey bristled. Was he implying *she* hadn't used common sense?

"It was a bit premature," he went on, "to advise Heather to initiate a lawsuit. Our courts are logjammed as it is with sue-happy people. The judges—"

"Who do you work for, Sheriff Hart?"

"What?"

"Who do you work for?" The challenge in her voice was unmistakable. "The citizens of this county or the judges?"

A waitress chose that unfortunate moment to arrive at their table, giving Bailey a chance to realize she didn't like the taste of the size-eight foot she'd just inserted into her mouth.

"I hope you aren't suggesting I'm a political puppet," Johnny said very quietly, after sending the waitress off with a request for iced tea.

"I didn't mean to—"

"Yes, you did."

Bailey stared at him. She'd never heard him speak so harshly.

"You thought I was censoring you," he said, "and you retaliated by sticking your fangs in my neck just like you used to do when we were kids. Dammit, I wish you'd quit doing that. I don't think I deserve it."

Johnny saw a blush creeping into her cheeks and knew he was right. She lowered her gaze and gripped her hands together in real agitation.

"I work for the *people*," he told her, just to set the record straight. "They feel free to approach me with their problems anytime, anywhere, because they know I'll listen. This is basically a poor agricultural community, Bailey. Unlike city folks, these people don't have corporations, organizations, and dozens of legal eagles behind them protecting their interests. So they come to me. I mediate their disputes and do the best I can."

"I'm sorry." She kept her gaze downcast. "I didn't mean to question your honor and insult you. I was . . ."

"Mad at me," he finished for her.

She didn't answer.

"Were you mad because Heather was sitting with me when you came in?"

"Please, give me a break. Why would *I* be jealous of that child?"

She still refused to look at him, though, and Johnny knew he was right. He swallowed a grin. It pleased him to discover she felt strongly enough about him to be jealous.

"As I was saying before I was so *rudely* interrupted," she continued. "I thought I was being helpful when I advised Heather of her rights. I didn't mean to start another war with you."

"I guess we have had our share of battles today." He laid his hand on her shoulder. She flinched, but he didn't take his hand away. "I realize we're coming from opposite ends of the law-enforcement game. You've spent your time handling the kind of hardened criminals I've never had to deal with and hope never to come across. Look, I know you're going to find that my methods of law enforcement are more laid-back than you're used to, but they work for me, and they work for the people."

A weak smile fought its way through her false mask of indifference and, once again, he knew he'd read her correctly. He didn't know whether to laugh or to ask the waitress to sprinkle his spaghetti with aspirin.

Bailey was strong-willed, stubborn, and courageous, and more tenderhearted than she let on.

She was driving him crazy, and he was loving every minute of the trip.

"You weren't wrong to advise Heather of her legal rights." He gave Bailey's shoulder a squeeze before letting go. "And I wasn't criticizing you for doing so. You just didn't have all the facts. Heather's aunt is the only family she has. A lawsuit could damage their fragile relationship beyond repair. Heather's still a kid. She may not realize it right now, but she needs her family."

Bailey blew out a long breath that ruffled her bangs. He was right about everything, so far. She had been jealous, though she'd rather die than admit it. She did perceive his attitude as too laid-back and his methods a bit antiquated.

"Maybe I am the wrong person for this job," she said slowly.

"No, you aren't. You'll get the hang of it."

"What if I don't?" She tilted her head back and looked at the ceiling. "What if I just can't fit in?"

"You will." He was determined she would. She had come back into his life and he was going to keep her there.

"Did we talk in *CAPITALS* when we were teenagers?" she asked, hoping to interject a lighter mood by imitating Heather's dramatic style of speech.

"I sincerely hope *NOT*."

Bailey looked at him, and they both burst out laughing. It felt so good to laugh, so good to restore an easiness between them, she failed to notice how the people around them glanced their way and smiled.

Johnny didn't realize they were being observed either. He wouldn't have cared if he did. He only had eyes for Bailey. At that moment she was the center of his universe. Her laughter pleased him more than the giving of gifts on Christmas morning.

His expression grew solemn. It was almost painful the way this fiery redhead got under his skin and sent his imagination up in flames. What would he do if she decided she wasn't cut out to be a small-town law officer?

"You look so serious all of a sudden." She combed her fingers through her long bangs, a gesture he was beginning to recognize as an anxiety signal. "Is something wrong?"

He was serious about wanting her. That's what was wrong. Move too fast, and he would scare her away. Move too slow, and he'd lose his mind. "My stomach just reminded me how hungry I am."

He caught the eye of a waitress, and she immediately came over to their table. "Maggie May, when are you going to quit this joint and run away with me?" he said jovially, noticing the tiredness in the woman's eyes.

Bailey sat back and listened to him flirt outrageously with the waitress who was old enough to be his mother. An amazing transformation came over the woman. She had approached their table looking as though her feet hurt and too many customers had been stingy with tips. By the time she walked away with their orders, she had a bounce in her step and a smile on her lips.

"I do believe you're still the biggest flirt in Profitt." Bailey turned and leaned back into the corner of the booth so she could see his face. "Tell me, Sheriff Charm, have you ever met a woman you *didn't* like?"

He raised an eyebrow. "Sheriff Charm?"

"Uh-huh." She grinned. "You're a magic toad, and you transform at will into Sheriff Charm."

"I thought a kiss was required to work magic on frogs and toads." His gaze lowered to her mouth.

"Not for you. The sight of any female will do."

"Ouch!" he exaggerated a wince. "You're trying to draw blood again." He turned to sit sideways and accidentally tangled one of his legs under the table with hers. She automatically shifted to put what little distance she could between them.

"Just answer the question. Have you *ever* met a woman you didn't like?"

He looked at her sleepily, for all his brown eyes were alert beneath their heavy lids. "I've met a few who didn't like me no matter how hard I worked at it, and I've met some who made liking them hard work." He shrugged. "I guess I'm a people person. Human beings fascinate me. We're full of wonderful contradictions. I enjoy the challenge of trying to discover the reasons for those contradictions."

"You sound like the psych majors I knew in college."

"I was a psych major."

"You're kidding! I didn't know that. Glowing reports of your victories on the college-football field were all I ever heard about."

He grinned, enjoying her astonishment. "Wanna come home with me and check out my degree?" And while she was there, he thought wildly, she could check out anything else she wanted, especially him.

"I'll take your word for it." In a humorous tone she added, "So, are you saying that flirting is your way of showing women you like them?"

He sighed. He honestly didn't consider himself a

flirt, and he wished she didn't view him as one. "I don't know if I'd put it quite that way. I'm nice to people, male or female. There's no harm in it. Being pleasant doesn't cost anything or take much effort, and it makes people happy."

She gave him a level look. "That philosophy would probably get you killed in the city."

"That's why I don't like cities."

"Touché, Sheriff Charm. So, you're a happy guy, and you want everybody else to be happy."

Johnny rubbed his index finger against his chin. Was she making an attempt to understand him, or was she being sarcastic? "I like myself and I like life," he said, summing himself up as simply as possible. "So why shouldn't I be happy?"

Why not indeed? Bailey wished she could say the same. Was his attitude genetically engineered? Or was it simply an adopted philosophy? Maybe Johnny was just one of those rare people with the gift of viewing the world and his place in it in a positive light.

The waitress returned with plates piled high with spaghetti, bowls of tossed salad, garlic bread, and tall glasses of iced tea.

They passed the time during the meal with pleasant conversation. Bailey hit upon a topic close to his heart when she questioned him about his home. He enthusiastically described the house he'd built on four acres of waterfront property on Lake George, modestly referring to it as his "little place in the woods." She was surprised to learn he had actually done a great deal of the work himself, and in the process had discovered that he enjoyed building things.

"I like working with my hands. I built shelves

and cabinets in the family room, and I'm working on the pantry now," he said with a hint of masculine pride.

Her gaze was drawn to his hands, and she smiled. Those big, powerful, square hands were busy demolishing a second portion of spaghetti.

He frowned thoughtfully. "The place doesn't really look like a home yet. In fact, it's kind of empty on the inside. You could help me with that."

Choosing furniture and knickknacks for his house seemed too personal and intimate to Bailey. It was something a wife should do. "Your mother always had good eye for decorating. Why not ask her?"

He laughed heartily. "Mom would love to get her hands on my house. I've had a devil of a time keeping her from taking over and filling it up with a lot of fancy, formal stuff that doesn't suit me. So how about it? Will you help me?"

Bailey absently drew an invisible pattern in the condensation on her glass as she considered the idea. She wasn't very domestic, but she had enjoyed fixing up her apartment in Cleveland. The task would require them to spend a lot of time together. That wouldn't be wise given the way he kept her physically stimulated and emotionally off balance.

"Maybe you should save the decorating for the person you choose to share your home and your life with someday." She felt compelled to add, "I'm not really a part of your life."

A gleam appeared in his eyes. "You're definitely a part of my life." He took her hand and interlaced their fingers. His palm was warm and hard. The inner surfaces of his fingers were slightly rough and hot. She tried to block the pleasant sensation shivering up her arm when he affectionately squeezed her hand.

"Only . . . only for a year," she whispered.

"You've always been a part of my life. You know me better than most people do. Say yes. I know you want to." The last was spoken as a silky challenge.

Oh, but she was tempted. She couldn't, though. She meant to refuse as she eased her hand from his, but found herself saying, "Let me sleep on it."

"Fair enough." He picked up the check and left a generous tip on the table. After draining his tea, he slid out of the booth. "I'd like for you to see the house. How about a quick tour?"

She remained seated, looking up at him. "Tonight?"

"Do you have anything better to do?"

"Not particularly." She thought about Cookie and Harry and their candlelight evening at home.

"Then come with me." He gazed straight at her. "You can see what you'll be getting into."

A current passed between them, an overpowering awareness that sizzled along Bailey's nerve-endings. The man was a menace to her senses in public. She didn't even want to think about how electric the tension could become in private.

"Come home with me, Bailey." His mouth widened into a coaxing smile. "You can look the place over. Then we can tell each other our deepest, darkest secrets over milk and cookies, just like—"

"—we used to," she interrupted. It was impossible not to return his smile. Impossible not to yearn for the easy friendship they'd known as children. And it was impossible to resist the sweet temptation of being with him just a little while longer.

"I have a feeling you're very good at organizing and manipulating people into doing what you want them to do," she heard herself say.

His dark brows arched mischievously. "Guess all those psychology courses paid off, huh?"

"Okay, I'll go with you to see your house." She slid out of the booth, dragging her wool coat along with her. "But I warn you, I expect your cookies to be chocolate chip and your secrets to be doozies."

An emergency meeting of the Saturday Night Bridge Club was being held around Cookie Hoover's kitchen table.

"I don't see the problem." Harry wasn't happy with the intrusion of his sister and brother-in-law upon his romantic evening for two. "You ought to see the goofy look on that boy's face when he talks about that little gal. My best guess is we'll all be picking out wedding finery before the year's out. Case closed. Marian, Frank, go home."

Cookie narrowed her eyes at him. "If you're going to act snippety, you can just forget . . . dessert."

Frank perked up. "Dessert?" He encountered "the Look" from his wife and added with a teasing smile, "None for me, thanks."

Harry made the obligatory contrite noises to Cookie, not wanting to press his luck by saying something that would cancel the best part of the night. His beloved's threat was a good one. Since he'd already eaten two slices of her cherry pie, he wasn't about to pass up the more heavenly dessert he'd been looking forward to. He crossed his arms and looked up at the ceiling, figuring he'd stay out of trouble that way.

"Bailey looked so down when she came home from work," Cookie said, getting up to refill everyone's cup with decaffeinated coffee.

Marian passed a packet of artificial sweetener to her husband. "That poor girl. I imagine it must have embarrassed her to death getting locked in a cell her first day on the job. You don't think she'll quit because of that, do you?" Marian looked upset.

"No, it would take more than that one incident to make her quit," Cookie said, putting away the coffeepot. "Bailey hates looking foolish, though. One summer she jumped off the high diving board at the pool and lost the top of her bathing suit. She was only ten and didn't have a thing to show, but she was so embarrassed, she wouldn't go back to the pool for the rest of the summer."

Harry got out his cigar and chewed on it thoughtfully. What did a lost bathing-suit top have to do with the possibility of Bailey quitting her job and leaving town before Johnny could marry her? Women. They could make the damnedest connections between unrelated ideas.

Cookie came back to the table and sat down. "The job is my concern. Bailey told me that she had to sit in the office all day with nothing to do. The look on her face when she described the day's events was . . ." She paused, laying her hand against her cheek. "She was disappointed. Very disappointed. That girl's always had more than her share of nervous energy. She can't sit still in mind or body. The busier she is, the happier she is. Too many days with little or nothing to do will drive her crazy.

"Her career is very important to her. If she isn't getting what she needs out of this job, she'll start looking for another one. Then she won't stay in Profitt long enough to fall in love with Johnny."

Cookie and Marian exchanged a stricken glance.

Everyone drank their coffee in silence for a minute.

Harry still didn't see what the big deal was.

Frank wasn't overly concerned either. He figured that what was meant to be was meant to be. That left his mind free to speculate on what kind of dessert Cookie had made.

The word "fate" wasn't in Marian's vocabulary. If one wanted something, one came up with a plan of action to get it. She picked up her cup and saucer and carried them to the sink. "There just has to be something we can do to keep Bailey in town. We need to come up with a plan."

"Do you have any ideas?" Cookie eagerly asked her.

Marian shook her head. She sat down at the table, distressed by her failure to come up with a plan of action.

Harry waved his unlit cigar. "If the girlie needs something to do, I say we give her something to do."

"Like what?" his beloved asked.

"Crimes to investigate."

Cookie laughed. "Oh, Harry, be serious."

"I am, my love." The cigar went back into his mouth. "I'm not suggesting we commit felonies. Just stir up a little mischief to keep her busy.

Invent a Peeping Tom, fake a few burglaries. Things like that."

"For heaven's sake, Harry," Marian said with disgust. "We can't go around committing crimes just so Bailey will have something to investigate."

"Sure we can. We'll ask our friends to cooperate. Can't really be a crime if we have permission to take things from our friends. We'll just be turning in false reports."

"We could get into trouble," Cookie said, though she looked almost convinced his plan could work.

"All we'd get is a slap on the wrist," he assured her. "No one would get hurt, and we won't be in any danger of going to jail."

Marian turned to her husband. "Harry's losing it. Takes after Uncle Pete. He had to be institutionalized because he was crazy as a bedbug. Thought he was a teapot and went around asking people to pour him out."

Harry glared at his sister. "Okay, then you come up with something. *You're* the one who wants to marry your boy off to the gal."

"I think we should sleep on it for a while," Frank announced.

"Good idea. Let's *all* go home and sleep on it." Harry nudged his brother-in-law's foot under the table and gave him a fair imitation of Marian's "Look."

# *Seven*

Bailey parked her car beside Johnny's black Blazer and got out. She had insisted on driving her own car to Lake George. That way she could leave whenever she wanted.

"That's some *little* place in the woods you've got," she said, walking over to where he stood waiting for her.

"Thanks," he said, grinning.

She nodded and turned to gaze admiringly at the two-story cedar-and-glass house, sitting in harmony with nature on a gentle slope above the lake. "I particularly like the half-circular window and skylights in the gable."

"I wanted natural light and a sense of openness for the second-story rooms." He took her arm to guide her along the snow-covered ground. "The deck extends around three sides of the house."

"Your home is lovely, and the setting is perfect for it."

"I like it."

She lifted her face and drew in a deep breath of the cold, crisp air. A chill wind moved through the trees, and above the moon was a pale crescent in the dark sky. "I'd forgotten how beautiful and peaceful it is here."

"Kind of magical, isn't it?"

The reverence in his voice made her smile. "Magical, yes. Spooky too. It's so quiet."

He glanced at her. "Missing the sound of sirens and traffic, are you?"

"Ah yes, the lullaby of the city." She laughed softly. "I'm afraid I do. Sometimes the quiet wakes me up in the middle of the night."

He shook his head. "Noise pollution was something I could never get used to when I was going to school in Cincinnati. Personally, I can't understand the attraction of a big city. To me it's just twenty-four hours a day of noise, exhaust fumes, crime, and too many neurotic strangers crammed together in too little space."

"Isn't there anything you like about cities?" she asked, amused by his country-boy snobbery.

"The availability of major-league sports." He unlocked one of the doors at the double-door entrance. As an afterthought he added, "And the theater."

"At least we agree on something."

"You still a Cleveland Browns fan?" He held the door for her.

She grinned. "You bet. Win or lose."

He switched on an overhead light. "This is the living area." He gestured to a wall of glass with sliding doors that opened to the deck on the north side. "It gets plenty of light during the day and provides a pretty view of the lake."

Bailey told him she was enchanted with all the open space and the stone-faced wood-burning fireplace that was the focus of the room. He was pleased when she commented favorably on the padded built-in benches that flanked the fireplace, creating a contemporary version of a classic inglenook.

"Let me take your coat." He helped her out of the garment and hung it with his in a closet by the entrance. Coming back, he took her over to the south wall to show her the shelves and cabinets he'd built. "TV, stereo equipment, and books."

"Very nice." She ran her hand over a shelf, impressed with the workmanship.

"Come on, I'll show you the bedrooms upstairs." He stopped on the way and showed her the half-bath located under the stairs.

A few minutes later they went downstairs again. Never, Bailey thought with amusement, had she seen a man so filled with pride over his home.

The master bedroom, she discovered, was set back in its own wing on the first floor. More windows and French doors opened onto the deck on that east side of the house. A wall of mirrored closet doors made the large area appear even more spacious.

The adjoining bath was a work of art. Bailey imagined the luxury of soaking in the sunken tiled tub at the end of a long day. The huge tub sat flush against a wide window that brought in the outdoors.

"It's fabulous," she said, following him into the kitchen. "I love how every room has a view of the woods and lake. You weren't kidding about the place being empty, though."

The only furnishings in the entire house were a reclining chair, a couple of wooden snack trays, and a freestanding hammock on a metal frame in the living area; a king-size bed in a black frame and another snack table holding a lamp in his bedroom.

"You can see why I need you."

"What you need is unlimited credit at a furniture store and the services of a good decorator."

He just laughed and hurried her through the U-shaped kitchen area, barely giving her time to glance at the ample counter space and built-in breakfast table.

"This is the laundry room and pantry."

She stood in the doorway and dutifully admired the large area and his half-finished pantry shelves. "It's a dream house, Johnny," she said. "A fabulous retreat from the world."

"I hope you'll come back during the day." He turned to face her. "Then you can really see how pretty the view is." His gaze flickered over her face before focusing on her mouth. He leaned closer to her.

Bailey read his intent and quickly moved back. She walked to the sliding glass doors in the kitchen and stared out, wishing she could see the lake, wishing she weren't having an anxiety attack over the thought of kissing him.

Johnny sensed she felt ill at ease now that the tour was over. He crossed to her and put his hands on her shoulders. She tensed, letting out a small gasp.

"I didn't mean to startle you." His voice was little more than a whisper. He noticed a flash of panic in her eyes as she turned her head to look up at him. Then her expression smoothed out like a calm sea. "Is everything all right?" he asked.

"Of course. I was just thinking."

"About what?"

She didn't answer him at first. She gazed back out into the night.

It was his touch that had startled her, and he thought he understood the reason for it. She was as aware of the powerful attraction between them as he was. It was always there, simmering just beneath the surface of polite conversation. It made his heart ache to know she was afraid of her feelings for him. And he wanted—no, he needed—to know the reason why. He instinctively understood, though, that he shouldn't rush her for an explanation.

"Cookies and milk," she said suddenly, her voice full of false animation. "You promised me cookies and milk."

"So I did." He dropped his hands to his sides. "Shall we go back to the living room? I'll build a fire."

"Sounds good to me."

Bailey followed him back to the living area and sank down on one of the padded benches flanking the fireplace. He didn't say a word while he arranged logs and kindling on the grate, and she was grateful for the silence.

She sat with her hands locked together in her lap. Her stomach coiled and tightened painfully. Never before had she considered herself a coward, but she felt like one now. She hated the feeling.

When he had the fire going, he stood up and gazed pensively down at her. He looked like a man sifting through burdensome thoughts. Turning on his heel, he moved a short distance away, then stopped and faced her again.

"Stand up," he said. "Turn your back to me and close your eyes."

"No. Why?" She hugged her arms around her waist.

"I didn't think you would." He rubbed his jaw while she waited for an explanation.

"One summer you and I went to a birthday party." He frowned. "It was Mary Beth West's party, I think. We were fourteen and fifteen. Remember?"

She shook her head, wondering what he was getting at. "No. What about it?"

"Someone suggested we play a game called Trust." He clasped his hands behind his back. "The game involved two people. One person stood a few feet behind another. The person in front was supposed to close their eyes and fall backward, trusting the other person not to let them fall."

She stared at him in confusion. "I don't remember playing that game."

"I do. Vividly. We paired up until we'd all had a turn with each other." He paused. "I was the only one you trusted that night."

"You were?"

He nodded. "You closed your eyes and didn't hesitate to fall right back into my arms, because you trusted me."

"So what's your point?" she asked in a tight whisper. It was obvious what he was leading up to. She wished she could prevent what was about to happen, but knew she couldn't.

"If I asked you to play the Trust game with me

right now, could you trust me not to let you fall?" His eyes bored into hers.

"I . . ." She couldn't hold his gaze. "That's a game for children." She hated the way her voice trembled.

A long minute passed in silence, then he said quietly, "We've grown up, Bailey, but you can still trust me. I would never let you fall."

She heard the assurance in his voice, and she believed him. In her soul she knew he was a decent man. A simple man in that he didn't seem to possess the kind of complicated inner self that tormented most people. And he didn't deserve to be troubled by her complications.

She raised her head and studied him, his shoulders a perfect resting place, his eyes that revealed his tranquil nature, his smile that melted the heart right out of her body. It was so easy to remember why she'd loved him as a girl. It would be so very easy to love him again.

Bailey winced at that last thought. Something within her was afraid to love him. She couldn't block out the fears that drove her to expect the worst from him, from any man.

"You can trust me," he told her firmly.

She didn't answer, though she couldn't argue with that. On some deep level she trusted Johnny. Just not enough.

"I'd never intentionally hurt you."

She couldn't argue with that either. But still she kept silent. Unintentional hurts and her own experiences with men looking at her with nothing but lust in their eyes made her cling stubbornly to her fears.

Johnny sat on the bench opposite her. "I'm not

going to pretend I don't want you. I'm not going to
pretend I don't notice that you're attracted to me.
It scares you to death. Every time I touch you, you
practically jump out of your skin. Why, Bailey? I
need to know why you're afraid of me."

"Johnny, there are things you don't know about
me," she whispered.

Her eyes had taken on a wild look, he saw. The
look of being trapped. And it hurt to know he was
the cause of it. He couldn't back down, though. It
was far too important to find out what he was up
against.

He expelled a long sigh. "I realize that. With
thirteen years gone between us, there's a lot we
don't about each other. That can be fixed, though.
If you can handle my secrets, Bailey Asher, I think
I can handle yours."

Curiosity filled her eyes. "Do you have secrets?"

"One or two." He doubted his troubled him as
much as hers seemed to trouble her. "Do you
want your milk and cookies before we start?" He
hoped the little ritual would make her feel more at
ease.

"Sure."

He got up and headed for the kitchen. When he
came back a few minutes later, she'd moved down
onto the plush blue-gray carpet and sat with her
knees drawn up, her back against the bench. She
was staring into the fire.

"Here you go," he said. She looked up, and he
handed her a glass. Balancing the plate of
chocolate-chip cookies with one hand and his
milk with the other, he lowered himself to sit
opposite her on the carpet. The small space between the two benches would have made a cozy

little nesting place, he thought, if the situation were different.

He set the plate between them, then grabbed a cookie and bit into it. Stretching his legs out, he braced his feet against the opposite bench, almost but not quite touching her hips.

Bailey chose a cookie and ate it without really tasting it. He was being so patient, she mused, letting her take her time to sort out her thoughts and emotions. "What do you know about working vice?" she finally asked.

"Not much." He raised his glass and drained half the contents before lowering it to rest upon his stomach. She smiled faintly when she saw the milk mustache on his upper lip.

"Lucky you." Her smile turned sad. "I know too much." She studied the oddly tender expression on his face. "It's exciting at first. You seek out crime and then pretend to be something you're not in order to make the bust. You have to be able to act well and forget you're a cop. You have to hide your emotions and switch gears fast."

She licked her dry lips and turned her gaze to the fire. "It doesn't take long for the thrill to wear off. It's an ugly job, you see, even when it isn't life-threatening." She paused to take a sip of her milk, although she really didn't want it.

"Every night I'd start pumping up as I got dressed to go to work. Sometimes I was supposed to be an upscale call girl, other times a down-and-out thirty-dollar hooker. On the job I had to be ready for anything from an angry biker swinging a tire chain to a group of pimps threatening to slice me up unless I went to work for one of them. I learned to talk fast, say the right words, know when to stall for time, know when to go on the offense as a defense, and to pray hard my backup team could get to me in time when things went wrong."

Johnny could see her struggling to maintain her outward calm. With a tremendous effort of will he controlled the need to take her in his arms, controlled a raging anger over the thought of her ever being in that kind of danger.

"You don't meet too many nice, ordinary citizens working vice. Busting prostitutes is especially hard. They talk about themselves in the third person because their reality is so horrifying. By the time they're thirty, they look fifty."

Bailey leaned over to set her glass on the hearth because her hands had begun to tremble. "It's hard not to absorb all that ugliness when you're standing on a street corner pretending to be a prostitute to bust johns. It doesn't matter that you're a cop. It's still degrading. You keep telling yourself it's just a role. It will be over soon, and you can go home and be yourself. But it isn't that easy. Because no matter how much you try to keep your role-playing separate from who you really are, you're in that situation. It's happening to you, and it's real."

"I'm sorry," he said quietly. More sorry than she would ever know. "I can see how it would change the way you look at men."

She nodded, still keeping her face turned to the fire. "After a while it starts to haunt you, to change you. You begin to assume the worst about people." Her voice shook as she went on. "Your feelings about men and intimacy change because you're constantly dealing with men who want to buy you, sell you, go to bed with you. Some of those men have wives and families. Some of them are the lowest scum on the face of the earth."

Slowly, she turned her head to look at him. In her beautiful green eyes he saw raw emotion. "I haven't dated, haven't let a man get close to me in a year." She continued in a ragged whisper that tore at his heart. "That's why I overreact whenever you touch me. It isn't that I don't want you. It's just that my feelings keep getting in the way. I'm scared of the intimacy. And I can't help it. I'm sorry, so sorry."

She wrapped her arms tightly around her knees. Emotions she'd held in check for so long were threatening to leak out as though she'd become a sieve. Inner muscles coiled so tightly, she couldn't have stood up without doubling over.

Johnny closed his eyes, feeling her anguish mingle with his own. Some things broken were not easily mended. He didn't know how to go about mending what was broken in her.

He opened his eyes and stared at her. He needed her so badly. And whether she knew it or not, she needed him.

Getting to his knees, he picked up the plate of cookies, setting it and his glass on the hearth.

"Bailey, look at me," he demanded softly.

She glanced up, expecting to find revulsion in his eyes. Instead, she saw concern and tenderness. She saw the reflection of herself and a desire that refused to be denied.

"Could you trust me?" He spoke so gently, so wistfully, she wanted to weep. But she hadn't shed a tear in front of anyone in longer than she could remember.

"Yes, I think I could." She lifted her hand to his cheek, rubbing her thumb over the milk mustache he still wore on his upper lip.

It was a small gesture to be of such significance. For the first time she'd voluntarily touched him. A flurry of emotions raced through him, and he struggled to keep them under control.

"Then do you think you could give an old toad a hug?"

He opened his arms. She hesitated, then slowly rose to her knees. Smiling shyly, she went into his arms, and they closed around her.

"I do trust you," she whispered, finding the perfect resting place for her head upon his shoulder.

"Bailey?" He nudged her face up with his fingers under her chin. She met his gaze. Her eyes gleamed more brilliantly than emeralds and she smiled. "Is it okay to hold you like this? You can tell me if you're afraid."

"It's okay. It—it feels good."

He pulled her closer against him, inhaling the wonderful, warm, womanly scent of her. He'd give anything to erase the nightmares of her past experiences.

"I couldn't take it anymore, Johnny," she said, holding him tighter. Words rushed out; she was unable to stop them. "I couldn't put my emotions on hold anymore when I was out on the streets. I was beginning to do stupid things, taking dangerous risks."

She poured out the story of the night she risked getting into the van, all because she saw the Baby on Board sign in the back window. He rocked back and forth with her as she told him how it made her physically ill to arrest married men.

"That's why I came here. That's why I needed the change of pace of working here," she finished, rubbing her face against his shoulder in a fight against tears.

"It's okay. You're here now, in Profitt, with people who love you," he murmured soothingly. He slid his hands up her back to thread his fingers through her silky hair. Tipping her head back, he gazed down into her face. "This is the best place on earth to find peace and to heal."

Something she saw in his eyes prompted her to ask, "Is that why you came back here to live? Did you need a place to heal and find peace?"

"Yeah." He smiled wryly. "It's a long story. I'll tell you about it sometime. But not now." He lifted a handful of her hair and watched as the strands slipped through his fingers. "I love your hair."

"You used to call me carrot-top."

"I used to dream about it that last summer you were here. You wore it long then, almost to your waist. I dreamed about how it would feel trailing over my skin as we made love."

He meant to ask her permission to kiss her. His intention was forgotten when he met her gaze. He saw his own need and desire shimmering in her eyes.

Johnny bent his head slowly, giving her plenty of time to pull away if she wanted to. He felt her stiffen slightly, but she didn't move. Awareness along with a second's panic flashed in her incredible eyes, then the panic was gone. Her sigh was long and shaky as his mouth brushed hers. And still she didn't break away.

The last time he'd kissed her was a memory. She had been a girl then. The reality of the woman made it impossible not to want more than a kiss. He felt the ache of his need for her through every bone and fiber. With infinite care he kissed her again and again until he was shaking.

The taste and feel of her soft mouth was better than a boy's memory. When her lips parted on a soft moan, he swept his tongue inside to mate with hers.

No, thirteen years hadn't erased his memories of her. With the fire crackling nearby and his own flames burning higher, the past rushed back to him full of the sweet longings of youth, the frustrations of innocence, and soul-deep dreams laced with magic and wonder. It was all there in a simple kiss. And more.

More because there was tenderness, which youth had no patience with. There was white-hot passion born of experience, and the maturity to differentiate loving from lust.

His mind accepted then what his heart and body had always known. He loved Bailey Asher.

Holding on to her as though she were a precious treasure, he sank down to the carpet while carefully drawing her onto his lap.

"Johnny," she moaned against his lips.

She was so soft and sensual. He drank deeply of her mouth as he sought out the gentle curves of her body with his hands.

A war raged inside Bailey. She'd been kissed by him, held by him, so many times the summer of her seventeenth year. The boy had been generous and passionate then. The generosity and passion were still there in the man. She welcomed those gifts even as she became frightened by the strength and hunger in him.

She dragged her mouth from his and drew short pants of oxygen into her lungs. His lips were at her throat, his hands on her shoulders, lowering her back onto the thick carpet. Panic welled inside her, and she started to tremble. His mouth came down over hers as he covered her with his body.

She squeezed her eyes shut, urging herself to trust him, willing her panic to go away. This was just Johnny. Her friend. Now and always. He cared for her, and he would never hurt her.

Bailey desperately wanted to surrender to his gentle touch, his heat. But her wounded emotions kept getting in the way, and the trembling in her limbs increased violently. Her fingers plucked spasmodically at the sleeves of his sweater.

It finally got through to Johnny that she'd stopped responding. He raised his head and stared down at her. Color had deserted her face, leaving her skin so translucent, he could see the tiny network of pale blue veins.

He swore silently and moved his hands to frame her face. "Relax. You're safe. It's okay, love. Everything's okay. I swear it. Look at me, Bailey."

She heard his calming voice, felt the soothing way his rough palms moved over her cheeks. His lips touched her temple, lightly, gently.

"Johnny?" Her voice sounded hoarse. She opened her eyes and saw the troubled concern in his gaze. Lifting her shaking hand, she placed the tips of her fingers alongside his jaw. "Oh, I'm sorry," she cried softly.

"Hush. It's okay." He touched his mouth to her temple again, her cheek, her chin. They were sweet kisses meant to soothe and calm. He eased his weight from her and lay down by her side, though he kept one arm around her waist as if he could not bear to relinquish all physical contact.

"I'm the one who should be sorry," he said. "I wanted too much too soon. Please forgive me."

She heard a quiver of uncertainty and remorse in his words and immediately felt the need to comfort him. Turning onto her side, she looked into his eyes and managed a smile.

"It's not your fault. I was enjoying being held and kissed." Her voice still sounded ragged, but was returning to normal.

"I'm glad. I loved the feel of you in my arms." Johnny drew her a little closer to his body and was pleased when she made no move to stop him. "I really am sorry things were happening too fast. The last thing I wanted to do was frighten you."

She lightly pressed her lips to his. "Your touch stirs me deep inside," she whispered against his mouth. "I just need some time. Just be my friend for now."

He looked at her and put all the love he felt for her into a smile. He wanted to tell her he loved her, but he doubted she would believe him. She might think it was only a line, so he could steal more than she was ready to give.

"Then come here, Bailey," he said, tugging her down on top of his chest. He could have sighed with relief when she readily complied and snuggled against him.

"We'll just hold each other for awhile, friend to friend. Enjoy a few kisses and caresses." His hand glided over her hair. "You won't give more than you can. I won't push you for more than you're ready to give. . . ."

The soothing, coaxing sound of his voice reached through Bailey's fears and bought him a little piece of her trust. She relaxed and found the perfect resting place for her head in the hollow between his throat and broad shoulder.

It felt nice being close to him, listening to the crackle of the fire, feeling the warm solidity of his body. He made her feel safe. How long had it been since she'd felt that way? She couldn't remember. He brought her buried senses alive. And she was grateful to know she *could* feel all those emotions again.

She wasn't ready to trust him completely, though. She couldn't allow her emotions to lead her into something she wasn't ready for. And she was far too disciplined to let a man get too close.

Those thoughts caused a sudden rise of dark panic. "I have to go," she whispered.

"Not yet." His fingers traced the line of her cheek and moved on to her lower lip.

"I have to leave now." She sat up and quickly got to her feet.

Concerned, Johnny raised up. "Is everything okay?" It wasn't. He could see her struggling to remain calm.

"I'm fine. Really. I'll see you tomorrow." When he started to get up, she held out both hands to stop him. "No, please, don't get up. I can see myself out. Thank you for a . . . thank you." She turned and fled.

Johnny didn't say a word. He didn't know what to say.

She flung open the closet door and grabbed her

coat. "It won't work," she called out softly as she shoved her arms through the sleeves.

"What won't work?"

She averted her eyes from his. "You and me. Us. I can't have a relationship with you. We could hurt each other so easily."

"You're wrong."

She shook her head and turned toward the door.

"Be careful driving home."

Johnny sat there watching her until she'd closed the door behind her.

Then he let out a weary sigh. Bailey didn't understand that she already had a relationship with him. Past. Present. Future.

She was just too scared to let him get too close. He had a feeling it was going to be tough breaking through the wall she'd built between herself and men. That wall had been carefully constructed over a long period of time. It wasn't likely to disappear just because *he* wanted it to.

Thinking back over everything she'd told him of her life for the past few years, he could understand how the lines between the roles she'd played and reality had blurred, making the world look threatening. He could imagine all too well the degradation and disillusionment any woman having to masquerade as a prostitute would feel. Just thinking about it made him hurt to the core of his soul for her.

Rebuilding her trust would take time. She would be on a constant watch for any misstep on his part, any telltale sign that he wasn't worthy of her trust. And it would be damned hard for him to take that day after day.

Her feelings and needs would have to take priority over his, he told himself. Her needs were greater than his.

Was that what loving someone really meant? he suddenly wondered. Putting someone else's interests, comforts, and needs ahead of your own without any expectation of getting something back? No reservations. No locked internal doors. No holding back. No holding grudges.

Johnny got a sick feeling in his stomach. He lay back down on the carpet and closed his eyes. Loving someone who didn't have much faith in the male of the species was going to be hard work.

Love was damned complicated.

# Eight

"I'm a closet detective," Bailey muttered the next morning, staring at the dingy walls of the storage closet—aka the Investigative Unit. "With nothing to detect."

Her daily calls to the elderly had been made. She had set up a case-management system in the hopes of someday having a case to manage. She'd had a nice visit, three cups of coffee, and two chocolate doughnuts with that sweet Deputy Tim in the Records Department. At the rate she was going, she was going to be the fattest, laziest, most claustrophobic investigative cop in Ohio.

At eleven o'clock, with nothing more than lunch to look forward to, she drew in pencil a big happy face on the far wall. Having dressed more casually for work that day in taupe wool pants, a beige cotton shirt, and comfortable shoes, she was able to put her feet up on her desk while doing a little target practice, shooting rubber bands at the happy face.

Twenty minutes later a knock on the door startled her. A rubber band flew out of her hand, and she almost tipped her chair over in her haste to get her feet back on the floor.

"Just a minute!" She opened her desk drawer, quickly raked rubber bands into it, and slammed the drawer shut. Jumping up from her chair, she dashed over to the far wall. Taking up a casual stance in front of her artwork, she put one hand on her hip and propped her elbow on a flat wooden shelf at shoulder level.

"Come in," she called, striving for a brisk tone.

Her heart sank when Johnny entered the room. It had been hard work, but she'd managed to avoid being alone with him all morning for three reasons. She didn't know what to say to him. She was embarrassed because she'd spilled her guts out to him the night before. And she was afraid he might want to start treating her like a girlfriend or something.

"What are you doing over there?" He set a small wicker basket on top of her desk.

"Hi! Nothing. Why?"

"What was that commotion?"

"What commotion?"

He stared at her a long moment, obviously curious about her odd behavior. "That noise I heard just before I came in. Sounded like something fell."

Bailey lowered her arm and drummed her fingers on the edge of the shelf while she considered an explanation. Inspiration struck. "*Oh*, you mean this noise." She pounded her fist on top of the shelf. "Just testing for sturdiness. Good wood." She pounded it again. "Very sturdy."

His heavy eyelids lifted for a moment, and she saw his brown eyes take on a sagacious look. He shook his head. "That's not the noise I heard."

"Hey, it's the only noise I've got going on in here."

Johnny's curiosity intensified. She was hiding something. He knew guilt when he saw it. Did it have anything to do with last night? With the way she'd been avoiding him all morning? Or the rubber bands he noticed scattered on the floor around her?

He took a step toward her. "Are you all right?"

"Just peachy," she murmured.

"Uh-huh." He grinned. "Did you have an accident with a box of rubber bands?"

A faint blush colored her cheeks. "Spilled a box of those pesky little things. Don't you just hate when that happens? I was just going to sweep them up. But I don't have a broom, though I think one used to live here. So, what can I do for you, Sheriff Charm—I mean Hart?"

Boy, would he love to tell her what she could do for him. Three strides carried him across her office. He stood in front of her and braced one hand on the wall beside her head. "For starters, you can explain why you've avoided me all morning."

"I've been busy?"

"Me too. I've been busy remembering the way you kissed me last night, and I would like for you to kiss me again."

"What happened last night was a fluke." She placed her hand on his shoulder, and he thought she was going to push him away. She didn't.

He leaned closer and inhaled the light scent of

her perfume and tried not to think about touching her just yet. "Was it a fluke?"

"Yes. It shouldn't have happened."

"Why not? We both enjoyed it."

She lowered her gaze as though carefully thinking over her response, seemingly unaware that she was stroking his shoulder with the tips of her fingers. The little caresses were driving Johnny crazy. And he was loving every second of it, because it was another small step forward.

Bailey knew she was not a timid woman. Neither was she a coward—except when it came to physical and emotional intimacy. She hated feeling that way. Hated the fear and confusion dwelling deep inside her.

She stopped staring at one of his shirt buttons and met his gaze straight on. "You're right. I did enjoy those kisses, and I am attracted to you. Maybe it's because we have a history of friendship, and I felt safe with you last night. At least for a while."

"Explain 'at least for a while.'"

She tried to edge away from him. He wouldn't let her. His other hand settled on the wall on the other side of her head.

"Please tell me what I did to make you stop feeling safe."

"It wasn't you," she admitted. "It was me. I haven't felt anything physical for a man in so long, and I'm having a difficult time dealing with that."

"We can deal with it together." He rubbed the side of her face. Shivers of pleasure traveled across her shoulders, and she instinctively leaned into his touch.

"I don't think so, Johnny." Her voice trembled.

"Holding hands and kissing in the dark in the backseat of a car won't satisfy you anymore. You're a grown man who won't be happy in a limited relationship with a woman.

"I might as well be seventeen again as far as intimacy is concerned." She smiled ruefully. "Curious but too scared to go too far sexually. Interested but unequipped emotionally to build a relationship. I'm not happy with those feelings. It's just the way it is." She lowered her gaze.

"It doesn't have to be that way. I meant what I said about not pushing you beyond the limits of what you're comfortable with." He stopped speaking and waited until she looked up at him again.

"I know you believe that now," she said. "Will you in a week? A month? Six months?"

"Yes." He smiled. "I've been told I have the patience of a saint."

"Not around me, you don't." She couldn't help smiling back at him. "It's impossible, Johnny."

"I don't think so. All I'm asking is for you not to push me away altogether. We could be very good for each other."

She shook her head. "I don't want to chance ruining the good friendship with you. I—"

Her last words were lost on his lips. The kiss was understanding and sweet. Bailey was shocked at her own eager response to be soft and willing. She couldn't control the urge to put her arms around his neck. Her lips parted, and she raised herself onto her toes to meet a new urgency in his kiss, claiming that urgency for her own. She loved the taste of him with all the old familiarity of the shape and feel of his mouth. She loved the way his tongue stroked against hers, and the low rumble of pleasure that came from the back of his throat.

But she hated the niggling doubts that crept out from the shadows in her mind. They were the same monsters that had destroyed her good feelings last night. She dragged her mouth from his and lowered her head.

Johnny rubbed his chin lightly over her hair. His heart was slamming against his chest as though he'd taken part in a decathlon. He could hear the thunderous beat in his ears along with the sound of their rapid breathing.

"Bailey, you are my best friend," he said, when he could trust himself to speak calmly and evenly.

She didn't look up. "I find that hard to believe. We've only been together for three days in the past thirteen years, and you always had a lot of friends."

He raised his head and lowered his arms to his sides. "It's true. I don't think time has anything to do with it, though. And yes, I have a lot of friends. I have friends with whom I share a common interest like baseball or football. There are people I'm friends with because we share some of the same memories of growing up in this town. Every one of those people knows some small aspect of me and views me from whatever perspective they're familiar with. But there isn't any kind of reciprocal expression of feeling and thought. None of those people have ever shared my inner life.

"But you have. You *are* my best friend. Nothing can change that. I want to keep seeing you," he finished in a voice so soft, it was hardly more than a whisper.

They stared at each other for a long moment,

and it was a toss-up who was more impressed with his speech. Bailey, because the sincerity of it had touched her deeply, or Johnny, because he wasn't given to making long speeches about himself and because he'd never tried to put his own feelings of lonely separateness into words before.

"I don't know what to say. . . ." she began.

"Oh, hell!" he mumbled, suddenly remembering why he'd come to her office in the first place.

"What's wrong?"

"I forgot something important." He turned on his heel and strode over to her desk.

"What?"

"It's not a 'what.'" He flipped back the hinged lid on the basket he'd left on her desk. "It's a who."

Bailey stared at him. "I beg your pardon?"

"Actually, it's a him."

She gasped in surprise as he lifted a tiny kitten from the wicker basket. The shiny black creature stretched out all four legs and yowled with protest over being so rudely awakened from his nap.

"What do you think?" He held up the kitten in both hands. The result of his late-night brainsorm squirmed its warm little body around and tried to scratch him.

"It's adorable!" A smile lit up her face. She walked over to join him beside the desk. He handed her the kitten, and she delicately stroked it under the chin. "What's his name?" She cuddled the kitten to her shoulder.

"I don't know. He's not mine." Johnny saw that the tiny creature was now wide awake and was chewing on the tip of Bailey's collar.

She frowned at him. "You're not taking this sweet little thing to the animal shelter, are you?"

"No, he just came from there. He's yours. You'll have to give him a name."

"Mine?" Bailey looked dumbfounded at the announcement, but she rallied instantly. "This is a joke, right?"

He shook his head. "He belongs to you."

She chewed on her lower lip. The kitten kept nibbling on her collar. "I can't have a cat."

"Sure you can. You always wanted a pet when you were a kid, but you couldn't have one because your dad was allergic to dogs and he hated cats."

Her eyes widened. "You remember that?"

"I remember everything about you," he told her in a low voice.

"I'd have to ask Aunt Cookie's permission since I'm living with her."

"Yes, of course." Johnny saw no reason to mention that he had already spoken with her aunt. Mrs. Hoover had readily agreed with him that Bailey needed something to love, something she could feel free to give affection to.

Bailey reached up and carefully pried the kitten away from her blouse. "A pet is too much trouble. I can't keep it," she said with a pang of regret. "You take him, Johnny. You've got a house and a—" She broke off when she saw that he wasn't paying any attention to her. He was looking at something over her shoulder, and she could see laughter building in his eyes.

"A little artistic expression?" he asked.

*The happy face.* Bailey bit back a groan. She'd forgotten about it in her delight over the kitten. "Target practice," she mumbled.

"With rubber bands."

"Uh-huh."

"Darling," he drawled, throwing an arm around her shoulders. "We've got to find something for you to do. Tell you what. Grab your coat, I'm going to take you to lunch. Afterward, you're going to ride over the county with me. We'll see what kind of mischief the populace is stirring up today."

Bailey wasn't about to pass up the chance to come out of the closet. She put the kitten back into the basket and grabbed her blazer and coat from the top of a low filing cabinet. Opening the bottom drawer, she took out a shoulder bag.

"Do you have an aspirin?" he asked.

"No." He started laughing when she formed her hand into a gun and pretended to shoot him. "A permanent cure for a headache."

"Let's go, pistol-packing mama."

Bailey froze for an instant. "What about the kitten? We can't just leave the poor little thing here alone. And by the way, I'm not keeping it."

Johnny picked up the wicker basket. "We'll take him with us. We can tape a little gold star to his chest and make him an honorary deputy."

"We can't take that cat on patrol," she protested. "Isn't it against regulations or something?"

"Like I told you, I'm the sheriff." He opened the door and winked at her. "I get to make the rules."

Wednesday morning Bailey was in her office writing reports on the calls she'd responded to with Johnny the day before. She put down her pen and sighed. Fifty percent of the calls they'd dealt with centered on "communicating threats." Generally, they involved two or more people in the midst of a verbal disagreement, with at least one of them making threats. Not one of the calls they'd responded to had come close to requiring real investigative work.

Johnny had taken her to Bob's Drive-In for hot dogs and curly fries, then had driven her all over the county to familiarize her with the three patrol areas. He had teased her, flirted with her, and treated her like a friend, a *very* affectionate friend. By the end of the shift her senses had screamed to life, and he hadn't even kissed her once.

In frustration, she'd gone home and blown off steam about her day to Cookie. Then she'd taken two aspirins, a hot shower, and crawled into bed.

Only the kitten had slept peacefully through the night.

"You want me to do what?" Bailey asked when Johnny walked into her office the following Monday afternoon. It was the same thing she'd said to him at least three times her first week on the job.

One morning he'd come into her office with a gallon of white paint, a brush, and blue prison overalls. He'd dumped them on her desk and told her to have fun painting her office. Only his quick reflexes had saved him from taking a paintbrush upside the head.

Once he ordered her to fill in for a sick bailiff in small-claims court.

And then there was the flasher who preyed upon female school-bus drivers. She'd ended up driving an empty school bus along a country road where the flasher seemed to prefer strutting his stuff. Johnny had hidden himself on the bus, gleefully singing "The Wheels on the Bus Go Round and Round."

Bailey sat back and stared at him. "You're kidding? You want me to do what?" she repeated.

"It's a good thing I'm a patient man," Johnny said, thinking it wouldn't hurt to remind her of that sterling quality. He sat down on the corner of her desk. "I want you to take a squad car and drive over to the convenience store four miles west of town. Look for a girl named Staci. She'll be wearing a red coat and jeans. She needs a ride to the county line, where a deputy from that county will be waiting to take her home."

Bailey frowned. "I didn't spend four years getting a degree in criminal justice and eight years working for the Cleveland Police Department to become a taxi service. Ask somebody else."

"Bailey, remember Hart's Law number ten?"

"Have a heart." *And give me a break*, she silently added.

He smiled with approval. "The poor girl drove over to Profitt on a date with her boyfriend. The boyfriend got mad at her for some unknown reason and left her stranded on the side of the road. Staci was smart enough to call the Sheriff's Department for help because no one is at her home to come get her."

"Fine. *You* drive her to the county line."

"I would if I could, dammit." His halo of patience was slipping. He mentally pushed it back where it belonged and kept going. "I've got to be in court in fifteen minutes, and I have no idea how long I'll be tied up there. Take my car." He pulled his keys out of his pocket and tossed them to her.

She tossed them back. "I'm not a taxi driver. Ask Tim to do it. He'll be thrilled."

"Tim's got the flu. He went home an hour ago."

"Ask someone else." She sat back and folded her hands over her stomach.

"I've already checked with everybody else. You're the only officer available."

He leaned closer and looked her straight in the eye. "What would you rather do? Spend forty minutes driving that girl to the county line, or spend the next four months investigating a rape and murder case when we find her body lying in a ditch on some back-country road?"

"Give me the damn keys." She held out her hand.

"That's my girl."

"Woman."

"Right." He stood up and came around to her side of the desk.

"And I'm not yours," she said, staring up at him.

"Right." He pulled her to her feet and ran his wicked gaze over her. "Have I told you that I love the way you fill out a uniform?"

"About a dozen times." She'd been wearing the tan shirt, brown pants, and black boots since her fourth day on the job. "Do I have to wear the regulation hat from hell when I drive your squad car?" Privately, she didn't mind, but she enjoyed giving him a hard time about it.

"Of course. You look cute in it." He closed one hand around the nape of her neck. She loved the way his palm felt against her skin. "Wanna go to a party with me Saturday night?"

"I'll see if I can fit you into my *busy* weekend schedule. There's this sheriff I know who keeps dragging me to furniture stores, you see." She slipped her arm around his waist, encouraging him to move closer. He did.

"Know how to keep a sheriff from charging?"

"Make him leave home without his Master-Card."

"And hide his checkbook." He wrapped both arms around her. "Have you named your kitten yet?" His voice was filled with tenderness, and she felt as though she'd just been caressed.

"No." Her gaze flickered to his mouth. She wet her bottom lip with her tongue. "He's adorable, but I don't know if I should keep him." What she really meant was that she adored Johnny, but she didn't know if she should give herself to him.

"Keep him." A sensual flame burned in his eyes, and he gave her a smile that sent her pulses racing.

"Johnny." She laid the tips of her fingers along the side of her face.

"What?" One of his big hands slid with tantalizing tenderness up her back to cup her head. The other traveled from her waist to rest just beneath the fullness of her breast.

"Nothing. Just . . . *Johnny.*" She raised up on her toes and kissed him with a passion that seemed to explode from hidden depths within her.

Johnny swallowed her small sigh of pleasure and kissed her deeply, possessively. She was so warm, so soft, so giving in his arms.

Pent-up desire raged between them. His mouth slanted over hers again and again, until he realized he could take no more without wanting to lay her down on the desk and make love to her. He forced himself to stop.

Drawing back, he gazed into her face. She was staring up at him with such sweet confusion. Her lips looked swollen and thoroughly kissed, and he wanted to kiss them again.

He allowed himself only to hold her tightly for a long moment, then released her and stepped back.

Bailey was shaken by her own passionate response, shaken and thrilled. It felt wonderful not to be so afraid anymore.

She met his gaze straight on. There was such stark need and hunger in his eyes. He wanted more. And so did she. That revelation stunned her. She moved backward and sank down into her chair.

"Give that kitten a name," Johnny said as he left the office.

Yes, Bailey thought, clasping her trembling hands together. It was time to give the kitten a name.

That evening the Saturday Night Bridge Club met at Harry's house. They voted to go with his idea. Between the former attorney's cunning and Marian Hart's amazing talent for orchestrating events and people, by midnight they had a workable plan of action and the volunteers to carry it out.

The sheriff took a call late on Tuesday, and when he hung up, he went to inform his detective that she was going to respond to an incident of armed robbery at Gant's Hardware Store.

Bailey was thrilled at the prospect of investigating and managing her first real case. She told him responding to calls such as communicating threats and second-degree trespassing didn't count, since those were incidents that technically didn't fall into her official duties as chief detective of the Investigative Unit. And that fight two nights earlier at Cole Wan's Bar and Grill had certainly turned out to be much ado about nothing. Armed robbery, however, was a case of a different color, one officially right up her investigative alley.

Johnny wasn't thrilled. He worked hard at discouraging inappropriate use of handguns and rifles in a rural area where such weapons were commonly owned by citizens. And he was sorely ticked at the sucker who'd pointed a gun at Duncan Gant, a jovial man his father's age whom he'd known all his life, a man who kept a special box of miniature candy bars by the cash register for kids.

When they got into Johnny's police cruiser, Bailey buckled her seat belt and told him, "Hit the siren and step on the gas. I want to reach the crime scene as soon as possible to protect the integrity of any physical evidence left behind."

Gant's Hardware was only four blocks away, and Johnny didn't see any need for such noise and speed in getting there, but he deferred to her judgment. She was the detective in charge, and her eyes were glowing with excitement. So he flipped on the siren and laid rubber peeling out of the courthouse parking lot.

"I wish we had a mobile crime lab," Bailey shouted as they roared down Market Street.

"Whatever for?" he shouted back.

"Analyzing trace evidence. Fibers, hairs, soil, that sort of thing. We'll have to send that kind of evidence up to the crime lab in Columbus."

"Ooookay." He whipped around the corner to First and saw a pedestrian crossing in the middle of the street. The pedestrian saw the squad car barreling down on him and took off running for the sidewalk. Johnny silently apologized for scaring the dippity-doo out of the poor old fellow.

All along First Street cars pulled over to the side and people rushed out of the buildings to see what was happening. If Johnny hadn't needed to see where he was going, he would have ducked down in his seat in embarrassment.

Bailey had the passenger door open and was half out of the car before he came to a complete stop in front of the hardware store. He shut off the siren and engine, then followed at a more sedate pace.

"Howdy, Johnny-boy!" The sixty-five-year-old proprietor of Gant's Hardware gave the sheriff a hail-fellow-well-met slap on the back. "I'm mighty pleased you got here so quick."

"Hello, sir. I'm glad to see you're okay." In fact, Johnny thought Duncan Gant looked awfully chipper for a victim of armed robbery. "What did the thief get away with?"

"Well, as I was just saying to your detective here, I was lucky. Yes sir, real lucky. I'd just sent Hazel—that's my wife," he explained, turning to beam a smile at Bailey. "Been married to that wonderful woman for forty-two years. Happy as clams we've been, living right here in Profitt.

"Anyway, Hazel had just taken the day's receipts to the bank. So all the fellow got away with was twenty-five dollars I had kept in the till, one gallon of paint—white interior latex—one paint-brush, and a box of candy bars. Come right this way, Miss Detective, I'll show you where it happened. Now I was standing . . ."

For the next hour Johnny was treated to the impressive and thorough manner in which Bailey conducted an investigation. She insisted on having Deputy Tim join them to secure the crime scene, and Johnny decided he'd have to give the boy a chance to get out more, when he saw how eagerly and proudly Tim jumped to do Bailey's bidding. He didn't let a single curiosity-seeker cross the hardware store's threshold. Bailey, Johnny noticed, managed to restrain her natural impatience as she interviewed the witness. She listened well, asked good questions, homed in on salient facts with precision, and took careful notes.

Johnny did a lot of jumping himself to her commands. When she ordered him to get the camera out of the squad car, he didn't argue. She made him take photos of the crime scene from every imaginable angle, including one of a grinning Mr. and Mrs. Gant with their arms around each other, since she'd denied entrance to a reporter from the local weekly newspaper. When she said to dust for fingerprints, he dusted everything in sight. Not a trace of potential evidence escaped Bailey's attention.

And the thing he was most proud of was that she treated Duncan Gant with dignity and respect, and as though the thief had gotten away with the man's life savings.

"So what do we have to go on?" Johnny asked her as they drove back to the station house.

"Not much." She sighed and pushed back her bangs. "No one saw the man enter, and no one saw him leave except the victim. All we've really got to go on is that the perp is a white male between the ages of thirty and fifty, dressed in jeans, black jacket, and ski mask. He drove off in a recent model red Toyota truck with mud covering the license plates. We can put out an all-points bulletin on the truck, but I don't believe it will do much good. What do you think?"

Johnny shrugged. "Doesn't make much sense to me. The perp waited too late to collect any real amount of money. If he was a resident of Profitt, he'd know what time of day Hazel takes the day's receipts to the bank."

"If he's not a county resident, he's probably long gone by now. He could have easily driven into and out of town without anyone paying attention. The courthouse draws too much traffic for a stranger to stand out."

Johnny looked at her and smiled. "Maybe what we ought to be looking for is a guy who has a room that needs painting and a big sweet tooth."

She laughed and shook her head. "I hate to say it, but I'm afraid Mr. Grant is you-know-what out of luck."

"Me too." And that made Johnny mad. He didn't like the thought of any sleaze ball getting away with waving a gun at one of his citizens.

# *Nine*

Harry glanced around the Harts' garage where they had just hidden the evidence of their first felonious venture in a cardboard box marked CHRISTMAS DECORATIONS. He congratulated himself on his stroke of genius for choosing this place as their storehouse. It was a pack rat's nightmare of old furniture, lawn equipment, cast-off toys, and boxed-up items Marian had saved during thirty-eight years of marriage. Without doubt, Harry Baskin knew he would have made an excellent criminal mastermind.

"Are you all set for phase two?" he asked his brother-in-law.

Frank paused in his self-appointed task of recording the items taken from Gant's Hardware in a small spiral notebook. "Yes. Johnny and Bailey are coming over to watch the basketball game with me. Frances Kerrey will give Marian her VCR tonight after their committee meeting at church. You and Cookie will rendezvous with the Pattersons in Mansfield and collect their contribution to the cause."

"Very good." Harry smoothed a wrinkle from the sleeve of his cashmere coat. "Try to keep the brats busy until the burglary calls come in."

Frank nodded as he stowed the notebook in a box of fishing tackle. "I'm having second thoughts about keeping the stuff in our garage. It's too close to home."

Harry sniffed indignantly. Amateurs, he thought. Frank had already deviated once from the master plan in adding that damn box of candy to the loot agreed upon. Now he was questioning Harry's genius.

"That's the beauty of it," he said, waving his cigar. "Johnny will never suspect his own family. And the evidence will literally be under his nose in a place he would never consider looking for it."

Frank shook his head. "I still say we're going to catch hell if Johnny finds out what we're doing." His words were steeped in gloom, though his expression didn't alter from its usual serene state.

"Well, he isn't going to find out, is he?" Harry rose majestically and headed for the door.

Bailey walked up the steps to the Harts' back door. As she stomped her feet to knock off a layer of snow, she glanced around. She had always liked this side of the white frame house best, with its wind chimes swinging from the awning, Mr. Hart's rose garden off to the left, a big shade tree and bird feeders on the right. Of course, the rose-bushes were covered for the winter, and the tree branches were barren. But the sight of them triggered the memory of pleasant summer evenings when the air was rose-scented and a soft breeze whispered through the leaves and tickled the wind chimes.

Bailey thought of all the Fourth of Julys she had spent in the Harts' backyard. The Hoovers and the Harts always had a cookout for family and friends. Everyone would fill up on hamburgers and home-made ice cream. The adults would sit in lawn chairs and visit, and the children would play games until dark. Then they would all walk to the community center a few blocks away to watch the fireworks display while the kids lit sparklers and twirled them in circles and boasted about whose was the best and brightest.

Happy memories of happy times. Those days were immeasurably better than the last five years. Until she'd come back to Profitt, Bailey hadn't fully realized just how bleak and miserable those years had been.

Compared to working as a vice officer in Cleveland, being a small-town law officer was a pleasure, a delight in many ways.

Bailey knocked and waited, suddenly looking forward to the evening. She had seen the Harts briefly several times since she'd returned to Profitt. They had greeted her warmly and had made her feel like a welcome member of the family who had been away far too long. She'd liked the feeling.

The Harts hadn't changed much beyond a deepening of character lines in their faces. Mrs. Hart still smelled of White Linen and wore a string of pearls with everything from suits to casual clothing. She was a petite dynamo with laughing hazel eyes and a mane of perfectly coiffured champagne-blond hair, "compliments," she'd told Bailey, "of the expert ladies at Rhonda's House of Beauty."

Mr. Hart opened the door. His sweatshirt was emblazoned with the words CLEVELAND CAVALIERS. Buddy, the sweet-faced golden retriever at his heels, was wearing a cap with the same logo, and his furry ears hung out from the sides. "Bailey! Come on in."

A blast of warm, fragrant air hit her as she was drawn inside. Bailey found herself on the receiving end of an affectionate smile and a big hug from Mr. Hart while the pooch thumped his tail and let out a happy bark. "It's good to have you back with us," he said, giving her another squeeze. "We've missed you."

"It's good to be back. I've missed you too." The truth of those statements produced a warm feeling in Bailey. She marveled again over how easy the Hart family had made it for her to slip back into a comfortable relationship.

Mr. Hart was just as she remembered, the exact opposite of his wife: tall, lean, and quiet. Like his son, he projected an aura of strength and calm that was most reassuring. His brown eyes revealed an uncommon inner tranquillity that had always intrigued Bailey.

"The game is about to start." He rubbed his hands together and declared, "It's party time. Let me hang up your coat." He helped her out of the garment and folded it over his arm. "Make yourself at home in the den. I'll duck out to the garage and get the snacks. You won't tell Marian about my private stash of goodies, will you?"

"I won't say a word," Bailey vowed with a grin.

"That's my girl." He patted her cheek, then left her standing in the kitchen.

Bailey went into the den and sat down on the sofa. The dog barked sharply, jumped up beside her, and pawed at her arm, demanding her attention. She stroked the retriever's back as she thought how little the house had changed on the inside.

The furnishings weren't new, but they were well cared for. There was a clean, fresh scent, as though everything had just been scrubbed and polished to perfection. Mrs. Hart's Waterford crystal took up every flat surface, and Bailey remembered having to move all the pieces to safety for Tackle Wackle, a rainy-day version of a wild indoor football game that Johnny had invented.

"So, you're a Cavs fan?" she asked, glancing down at Buddy. His tongue lolled out in a canine grin. She took that for a yes. "Who do you think will win tonight? The Cavs or the Chicago Bulls?"

"The Cavs, I hope," Mr. Hart said, coming into the den. "The Bulls are going to be tough to beat, though. They were the best team in the NBA last season." He dumped his armload of junk food on the coffee table, then sat down beside her and reached for a bag of chips.

"That's true," she said. "The Cavs are impressive in their own way but a little conservative on the court." Bailey helped herself to a handful of potato chips. "The Bulls play rough. Nothing intimidates them. And they've got Michael Jordan. Did you watch the play-off game between the Bulls and the Knicks last season?"

"Yeah, those Bulls are purty darn good." Frank popped a chip into his mouth and sighed contentedly.

"I think they could have won the play-off if Jackson hadn't got himself ejected off the court near the end of game four." Bailey fed the golden retriever a chip. Buddy wolfed it down, then he laid his big furry head in her lap.

"Heard you had a little excitement down at Gant's Hardware this afternoon."

"I guess you could say that," Bailey answered, eyeing with interest the cupcake he was unwrapping. It had chocolate frosting.

"Think you'll catch the fellow who robbed poor old Duncan?"

Bailey shrugged. In spite of the interest she heard in Frank's voice, she didn't feel she should discuss the case with him. She stuck to a non-committal response. "Based on what little evidence we have now . . . it's hard to tell."

"Well, I wish you luck."

"It's the suspect who'll need a little luck," she said dryly. "If Johnny gets his hands on him, he'll string the guy up by his thumbs for daring to point a gun at Duncan Gant."

Frank went into a coughing fit. She grabbed a can of cola, popped the top, and handed it to him. "You okay?" she asked, when he calmed down long enough to take a gulp of the drink.

"I'm fine." He smiled weakly. "Just had a cake crumb stuck in my throat. So, how do you like your new job?"

"It's been interesting." Bailey unconsciously stroked the dog's back as she spoke. "Being a small-town law officer is vastly different from what I imagined. The job is more people-oriented, and that's a challenge for me. I'm afraid I've spent too many years dealing with hardened criminals best described as amoral to be any good at the kind of work the Sheriff's Department handles. I tend to be overly suspicious. I don't have Johnny's patience and tolerance."

Frank patted her hand. "That's understandable. You've seen humanity at its worst and have come to expect the worst. Puts a big dent in your faith in people. It may take you a while to adjust, but I think you'll find that here in Profitt folks are better than they seem. Don't worry, little Bailey. You'll get the hang of the job."

She smiled. "I hope so. I've learned a lot just from observing Johnny. He's a good sheriff. Straightforward, fair, patient, compassionate. He has a gift for seeing the best in people, and I envy him for that."

"His mother and I are very proud of him." Frank's eyes crinkled at the corners in a devilish smile. "Johnny is glad to have you back in town. I think he missed you more than he realized. The two of you were always so close. Especially that last summer you were here. Marian and I were convinced you'd be our daughter-in-law someday." He looked at her affectionately. "You won't hold it against an old man for clinging to that hope, will you?"

Bailey didn't know what to say at first. Then she laughed a little. "That's very sweet of you. But Johnny and I are just good friends." It was true enough. She was well aware that he wanted to become her lover. But love and marriage? No, she doubted the thought had crossed his mind.

"All right." Frank clapped his hands. "The game's starting."

*Marry Johnny.* Images and thoughts swirled

through Bailey's mind, stirring up hidden and long-forgotten emotions. Like most young girls at age seventeen, she'd dreamed of one day having a husband, a home, a family, and her career. Funny, back then she hadn't been able to picture a life with anyone but Johnny. Foolish romantic notions of having it all had been burned away after a few years on the police force. Nothing but the ashes had been left by the time she had resigned, and she hadn't been able to imagine herself married at all.

*Marry Johnny.* Once again the words swept through her mind like ocean waves pounding against the shore, pounding home a persistent message. For several moments Bailey surrendered to the temptation of wondering what it would be like to be Johnny's wife, to share a home with him, to work side by side, to create a family, and to love and laugh together for a lifetime. The tide of her thoughts crested, bringing a painful longing in its wake, and she suddenly felt threatened. Marrying her best friend was too ridiculous a notion to consider. Johnny didn't love her, at least not that like that, and she certainly didn't love him.

She didn't want to fall in love. Now now. Not with Johnny. Not ever. If you loved someone, he could hurt you. Hurt you in ways no one else could.

Barely aware of what she was doing, Bailey removed the cap from the dog's head and put it on her own. Then she stroked his head in an instinctive need for contact with another warm body to calm the riot of confusion within her.

A short while later Frank and Bailey were so

caught up in the game, they didn't hear Johnny come in. Neither did the dog, who was snoring softly, still using Bailey's lap for a pillow.

Johnny leaned against the jamb in the doorway between the kitchen and den, his gaze locked on Bailey. She was curled up on the sofa, the dog on one side of her and his father on the other. She was absently rubbing Buddy's furry ears, and she was wearing his cap. Her eyes were wide and sparkling with excitement.

Johnny was stricken by an almost irresistible urge to kiss the tip of her nose, her cheeks, her stubborn chin, and last of all her lips. It would give him great pleasure to give special attention to the smear of chocolate in one corner of her mouth.

He shook his head. He hadn't been so swept away with longing, hadn't felt such a ridiculous surge in hormonal level since his adolescence. In fact, he was willing to bet his sheriff's badge that Bailey had caused his reaction then too.

A knot of uneasiness settled in his stomach. Waiting for her was becoming more and more difficult. She worked by his side during the day and lived in his dreams at night. And he was just too damn old to be satisfied by dreams of that kind.

Johnny didn't know how much longer he could keep from showing the love he felt for her. But he had to, or he'd risk scaring her away. She needed time to learn she could trust him completely. He didn't want to fail Bailey or himself by rushing her into something she couldn't handle emotionally.

Their relationship was inevitable. Inevitable and right. Johnny had never thought much about destiny before, but now he truly believed that his lay with this woman his best friend had become.

Finally sensing his presence, she turned her head and looked at him. A slow, sweet smile formed upon her lips. "Hi," she said. Her voice was as soft as a cloud.

He smiled. "Looks like you two started the party without me."

The golden retriever lifted his head, barked out a greeting, and bounded off the sofa. He pranced across the room with eager sprightliness. Johnny bent down to scratch the dog behind his ears.

"About time you got here, son," his father said, getting to his feet. "I was beginning to think I was going to have this pretty girl all to myself tonight." He moved to a chair closer to the TV.

"Sorry I'm late." Johnny straightened and walked over to sit beside Bailey. The dog crawled up beside him. "What's the score?"

"The Bulls are ahead by six points," Bailey said. "The Cavs keep leaving the door open just a crack and—" She turned to look at him, and whatever else she intended to say was lost when she met his gaze.

Emotion swirled through his brown eyes, mesmerizing her. She wasn't aware he had lifted his hand until his thumb gently touched her lower lip.

"You have a smear of chocolate right there," he whispered.

Bailey was conscious only of the feel of his thumb rubbing across her lip. His touch was haunting, promising.

Caught in a spell neither of them had intended, she tilted her head back, and he bent slowly toward her. Their mouths were a scant two inches apart when Frank let out a scream. "Man, what a comeback!"

They sprang apart guiltily.

"Wasn't that a beautiful cut right across the middle for a hoop?" Frank beamed at them. "Did you see the way he stepped back and hit that jumper?"

"Uh-huh." Bailey nodded vigorously.

"Great," Johnny murmured. "Yeah, that sure was one . . . uh, great shot."

Bailey felt her face flaming scarlet. Sinking back against the soft cushion, she pulled the baseball cap almost over her eyes.

If Mr. Hart hadn't yelled like that, she would have been kissing Johnny as though she were a randy teenager caught up in a hormonal maelstrom. Where was the control she prided herself on? Her common sense? She had neither where Johnny was concerned, she decided unhappily.

For a while Bailey watched the Cavs game in an erratic fashion. She saw images on the screen, heard cheers from the spectators and occasional comments from her companions, but most of all she was aware of Johnny, of every breath he took, of every movement he made, no matter how negligible. With her peripheral vision she saw him dart little looks at her, looks she refused to return.

An hour later the beeper Johnny carried went off. "Damn thing," he muttered, and Bailey smiled as he left the room to call the dispatcher. The "damn thing," as she'd often heard him call the beeper, had a range wide enough to cover the county, so there wasn't anywhere he could hide when he was off duty.

He was back in a few minutes, carrying both

their jackets. He appeared agitated, an unusual condition for him, Bailey thought. "What's up?"

"Two burglary incidents. Put your coat on," he said, tossing the garment into her lap. "Let's go."

"Should I stop by the house for my gun and badge?" she asked, rising quickly and shoving her arms into her jacket.

"No. You won't need them."

Frank stood up. "Whose houses were broken into?"

"Frances Kerrey's and the Pattersons'." "Grim" best described Johnny's tone of voice.

"Oh, that's too bad," his father said sympathetically. "Your mother was supposed to drive Frances to and from the church meeting tonight, so I'm guessing she wasn't home at the time. Sure hope the Pattersons weren't home either."

Johnny frowned. "I don't have all the details yet. Sorry, Dad, but we've got to go. See you later." He turned on his heel and headed for the door.

Bailey followed him. In a way she was grateful for the calls demanding their attention. Taking care of business would keep her mind off her raging hormones and disturbing emotional reactions to Johnny.

The second the two were out the door, Frank wiped a hand across his brow. He wished he'd never agreed to go along with his brother-in-law's harebrained scheme. Johnny was going to have their guts for garters if he ever found out they were involved.

Would he have to share a cell with Harry if they went to jail? he wondered. Lord above, he hoped not.

Frank began gathering up the remains of their

junk-food feast because Marian would be home any minute. If she walked in and discovered his illicit goodies, she'd kill him. He sighed. At least then he wouldn't need to worry about being stuck with Harry for a cellmate.

Johnny was in a foul mood. A crime wave had hit Profitt. For the last three days and nights he and Bailey had responded to at least a dozen reports of a Peeping Tom who seemed to prefer peeping at grandmas in their nighties. He couldn't stand the thought of some sicko running around town scaring sweet old ladies he had known all his life. And then there were the burglaries. VCRs and jewelry were disappearing faster than a minimum-wage paycheck. His own parents had been relieved of their VCR and his mother's fine jewelry, increasing Johnny's rage a hundredfold.

At 1:00 A.M. Saturday morning Johnny and Bailey were patrolling the town in his police cruiser. He glanced at her and saw that her face was turned toward the passenger window. He knew she was watching for any hint of movement in the dark as he slowly drove through a residential area.

Crime had stalled their relationship, and he hated that as much if not more than the crimes themselves. In the past seventy-two hours they had spent more time together than most married couples do in the same time frame. There wasn't anything exactly wrong with the hours they were together, except that they devoted themselves to business. Every day they chased down leads that went nowhere. Every night they responded to calls and investigated incidents until he dropped her off at her aunt's house.

So it wasn't like they were dating or anything. A touch, a look, a rare kiss, were all they had exchanged for three blasted days. And he didn't have a single clue whether she trusted him enough yet to let him get closer to her.

In his frustration he'd even considered the possibility that he was deluding himself in thinking she would ever want anything more from him than friendship.

Johnny wished he had someone to talk to about it. He didn't want to broach the subject with his parents—his mom would only get upset on his behalf, and his father would probably tell him that what was meant to be was meant to be. Not exactly the helpful hints he needed. Mrs. Hoover was out too. She was Bailey's aunt, and it wouldn't be fair to discuss it with her. In fact, he couldn't discuss his problem with anyone, because he would be betraying a confidence about her fears.

Worst of all, he couldn't ask his best friend for advice, because she was the person he needed advice about.

"It's too bizarre," Bailey suddenly said.

Johnny glanced at her again. He was tired of hashing over their dead-end investigations, but he sensed she had something on her mind and needed to think it over out loud. "What's too bizarre?"

"I don't know. There's just too many things about these incidents that don't make sense." She picked up the thermos lying between them on the seat and poured coffee into a cup. "Want some?"

"Yeah." He took the cup she held out to him.

When she had poured herself a cup, she said, "There probably isn't any use in going over the same old ground, but there are some things that bother me. First, all the burglary victims are senior citizens. None of them was home at the time of the robbery. The suspect must be someone who is familiar with their everyday routines and activities. Therefore, he or she must live here in Profitt, have constant contact with those people."

"That bothers me too, to think it could be someone they know and trust. Hell, it could be somebody *I've* known all my life. I hate that. Really hate that."

Bailey swallowed a mouthful of coffee. "Second, there were no witnesses. None of their neighbors saw or heard anything out of the ordinary. And there was not one sign of forced doors or broken windows in any of the burglaries. Only two out of the seven victims admitted to leaving a door unlocked. So how did the suspect enter the other five houses?"

"Beats the hell out of me." He sighed wearily and drank down half his coffee.

"Then there's the Peeping Tom victims."

"What about them?" he asked, frowning.

"Every one of those ladies told the exact same story."

"So what? The same thing happened to all of them."

She shifted around to face him. "Think about it," she said irritably. "A dozen people experience the same event, and not one of them gives a different version of what they saw. That's damn odd, because individuals perceive things in their own way. For instance, they all described the suspect as being of medium height. Mrs. Lane is almost six feet all, and to her a man of the suspect's height might appear to be short. A five-foot woman would probably describe the same man as being tall."

Johnny was shocked. "Are you saying they're lying?"

She ran her fingers through her bangs and let out a long sigh. "I hate to say it, but that thought has crossed my mind more than once. Maybe it's just a case of loneliness and boredom. I realize they're all dear, sweet ladies, but they all live alone. Who knows? Maybe one actually saw a man peeping in her window or thought she did. Maybe she told the others, who thought it was exciting."

Johnny considered that logic and found it deeply disturbing. He had known and liked those ladies all his life. It had never dawned on him to question the ironclad sameness in the descriptions of the incidents and the suspect. But Bailey, new in the community and not personally involved with any victims, had been much more observant than he.

"So what do you think?" she persisted.

He didn't answer immediately. Instead, he turned the corner, drove the cruiser to the end of a dead-end street, and stopped. He switched off the headlights, because there was a streetlight nearby, but kept the engine running for heat.

After draining the last swallows of coffee, he stared out into the dark.

"Are you angry with me, Johnny? Maybe I'm way off base in my thinking. After all, I don't know these people like you do."

She sounded defensive, and he knew that meant she was upset. "I'm not angry with you. I'm angry with myself for not paying as much attention to details as you have, for not being even a little bit suspicious. What I think is that your theory could very well be the right one."

She was silent for a moment, then said kindly, "I imagine it would be difficult to suspect the motives of one's first-grade teacher."

Johnny shook his head wearily. "You've got that right." He looked at her. "What have we been doing for the last three nights? Chasing a nonexistent voyeur and providing attention to a bunch of lonely people? If that's the true situation, how are we going to put a stop to it?"

She shrugged. "Don't ask me. You're the one who's good with people, Sheriff Charm. You're the one who holds a degree in psychology. I'm just a cop who's real good at being suspicious of my fellow human beings."

To her amazement, he started to laugh. He laughed so hard, he bent over and laid his head on the steering wheel. "Mind sharing with me whatever you found so amusing?" she asked tartly, once he'd calmed down.

"Me. You. Us."

"I don't understand."

"I'm not suspicious enough, and you're too suspicious. I trust people until they prove I can't trust them. You're just the opposite. Together, we make quite a pair."

"Yes, I guess we do. Maybe we can learn something from each other and reach a happy medium," she said lightly.

"Do you know one?"

"Pardon?"

"A happy medium. We could call her up and have her consult the spirits for guidance in tracking down our burglar."

Bailey said on a gurgling laugh, "You're getting punchy. Shall we call it a night?"

On a pun roll now, he couldn't stop. "Sure, we can call it night. It's dark outside."

"You're definitely punch-drunk, Sheriff. Let's go home."

"I don't want to go home yet," he said, turning serious. "Know what I want to do?"

She set her empty cup on the dashboard. "No, what?"

"Talk, Just sit here and talk."

"Okay."

He turned off the engine. Bailey waited for him to say something, but he just stared at her and remained silent. "I named the kitten," she blurted out.

She watched a slow smile spread across his face. "You did?"

"His name is Trouble." *Big Trouble.* Just like her feelings for Johnny.

He wanted to kiss her. He took a deep breath in an effort to control his elation. "You're going to keep him." If she kept the kitten, maybe she'd keep *him* too.

She folded her arms. "Yes, I guess we're stuck with each other."

"Do you still want to go to the party with me?" Johnny glanced at his watch, a good excuse not to look at her beautiful mouth. "In exactly seventeen hours and ten minutes?"

"What about being on call in case our burglar strikes Saturday night?"

"We need the break." What he really meant was that they needed a chance to be together off the job. They needed to work on their stalled relationship. "I'll have a couple of my part-time deputies cover for us."

"Sounds good to me. Will I know anyone at the party?"

"Oh yeah. Several of the kids I hung out with in junior high and high school came back to town after college. I know you met most of them at one time or another. And there's the Rollinses, who are giving the party. You don't know Anne Rollins. She's from Kentucky. But I'm sure you'll remember her husband, Blake. Big blond guy. Played baseball with us. Great pitching arm. His fastball was pure poetry in motion."

Bailey snorted and stared out the window. "I remember *him*. He was fast all right. Fast with the girls. He pitched more come-on lines than he did baseballs. I almost broke his great arm once for copping a feel of my behind."

"That's him. A real hell-raiser on and off the field."

"I pity his poor wife. If ever a man was born to stray, it was Blake. I'll bet he's a gynecologist."

"Nope. He's a minister."

She whipped her head around to look at him. "No way!"

"Yes way. Blake confines his hell-raising to the pulpit every Sunday." The laughter he'd been holding in check filled the car.

"I can't believe it."

Johnny crossed his heart. "I swear it's the truth.

Blake is a faithful husband and a doting father to his children. He and Anne are very happy together." Johnny was glad for the opportunity to work in that point, because he had a feeling Bailey hadn't been around too many happily married couples, and marriage had been on his mind a lot lately.

"They have two of the cutest little boys you've ever seen," he continued, warming to the subject. "Ages four and five. I coached them in a peewee-football league last fall. David, the five-year-old, already shows potential. He has good hands and he's fast. In about ten or eleven years he could be Profitt High's star wide receiver."

"A wide receiver just like you, eh?"

"Shoot, he'll probably be better than me."

Bailey huddled inside her jacket, because the cold was already seeping into the car. "You were good, Johnny. Damned good. It's hard to believe you didn't go professional."

"Are you disappointed I didn't?"

From the sharp edge in his voice Bailey realized someone who mattered to him must have been very disappointed, and he had been hurt by it. She wondered who.

"Not at all," she answered carefully. "I was surprised, though. You never talked about doing anything else the whole time we were growing up. What happened to change your mind?"

"I got scared." He squirmed and stared out the windshield.

Of all the reasons he could have given, fear was the one Bailey would never have considered. She knew what it must have cost his masculine pride to admit it.

"I've never told anybody that before. Never even said it aloud. It's getting cold in here." He started up the engine but made no move to drive away.

"You don't need to talk about it if you don't want to." She reached across the seat and touched his hand.

He threaded his fingers through hers and met her gaze. "I'm not harboring some deep internal wound over it."

"Because coming home healed you?" she guessed, remembering what he'd said to her that night at his house about the healing powers of his hometown.

"Yeah." He smiled. She smiled back.

Silence stretched between them for a few moments, then he spoke. "By the end of my senior year of college, I was a third-round draft choice, and my agent was negotiating a contract for me with the Los Angeles Rams. Before I signed the contract, I went to L.A. to check it out. I hated the city. I've already told you how I feel about places like that."

"'Noise, pollution, and too many neurotic strangers.'"

"You do listen real good, brat." He grinned and squeezed her hand. "While I was in L.A., I was invited to party with celebrities, sports legends I admired, and more beautiful women than I'd ever seen in my life. That night I saw things I'd only read about or had seen in second-rate movies. No less than half a dozen of those beautiful women offered themselves to me. They didn't know who Johnny Hart was, and they didn't care. All that mattered was that I was going to be an L.A. Ram. Drugs were as available as beer, and I saw men I'd admired and respected think nothing of indulging. Scared the hell out of me."

Bailey's heart went out to him. She knew firsthand how ugly things like that could be.

Johnny smiled wryly. "That started me thinking. Two hundred thou a year wasn't worth living in a place I would hate, or being constantly surrounded by people I'd never be comfortable with or be able to trust, or having my privacy invaded by the press. Money and fleeting glory for damn sure wouldn't be worth the risk of ending up a physical wreck of a has-been.

"Everybody thought I was crazy to turn my back on the opportunity to play for the Rams. The woman I was engaged to told me to take a hike. Turned out she was more interested in my future earnings and the chance to be a celebrity's wife than she was in me."

Bailey was stunned. She had never heard a word about him being that serious about a woman. "I'm sorry. Did you love her very much?" she asked quietly.

"Oh, I thought I did at the time. I know now that I was wrong." He raised their entwined hands and brushed a kiss over her knuckles. "Now you know my deepest, darkest secrets, and I know yours," he said, and switched on the headlights.

A deep silence descended within the small confines of the police cruiser. He didn't know all her secrets, Bailey thought as they pulled away from the curb. There was one more she'd been keeping even from herself.

She'd fallen in love with her best friend.

# Ten

It was midnight when Bailey and Johnny finally left the Rollinses' "three alarm chili" party.

"Did you have a good time?" he asked when they were settled in his car.

"I had a wonderful time. The chili was truly alarming, the beer was cold, and I enjoyed your friends. I was surprised by how many people remembered me and how warmly they welcomed me back."

He nodded. "They're nice people."

"Yes, they are. And so are you." She leaned over and kissed his cheek. He made an odd sound, and when she drew back to look at him, his gaze dropped to her mouth. In his eyes she saw a longing that fueled her own.

"Where do you want to go now?" he asked.

She took a deep breath and let it out slowly. "I want to go home with you." She thought her voice sounded remarkably strong and clear for a woman who was about to take a radical leap of faith. "I didn't bring an engraved invitation with me. Will you accept an oral one?"

Johnny went perfectly still, remembering the night he'd told her he wouldn't touch her without a formal request from her. Was she really saying she trusted him that much? He forgot to breathe as hope filled him up.

He exhaled slowly, closing his eyes for a moment and then opening them to stare at her. "Are you certain? You're looking at a man who desperately wants to make love with you." A man, he added silently, who desperately wanted to love her for the rest of his life.

She touched the side of his face and smiled. "Completely certain." Her fingertips slid down beneath his chin, and he tried to subdue his elemental response to her gentle caress. "If you want, I'll get out of the car and play the Trust game with you to prove it."

Without a word, Johnny started the engine.


They stood facing each other in the middle of Johnny's living room.

"Do you want me to start a fire?" he asked.

"Later, maybe." The fire roaring inside Bailey was more than enough for the moment.

"A glass of wine?"

She shook her head.

"That's good." He grinned sheepishly. "I just remembered I don't have any wine. I can offer you milk and cookies, though."

Bailey again shook her head, then she couldn't help laughing because he looked so nervous. It amazed her that he was and she wasn't. "A hug would be nice," she suggested.

He sighed and walked over to her. "Hugs I have plenty of."

She wrapped her arms around his waist, and as he held her tight, she became aware of him in every fiber of her body. Looking up at him through her eyelashes, she said, "That's good, because I've become addicted to your hugs. You're a champion hugger."

"You're not a bad hugger yourself. In fact, I think you're well on your way to being champion material." Johnny smiled down at the woman in his arms, and the trusting way she smiled back vanquished all doubts from his mind.

"You're not afraid anymore, are you?" he asked softly.

"No. Not with you. With you, I'll never be afraid again." Nothing she could have said could have moved him more or sounded more eloquent.

He slid one hand along the curve of her hip in slow delight. He loved everything about her, the way her long eyelashes lay upon her cheek, her snippy little nose and stubborn chin, the courage it must have taken for her to overcome her fears, the translucent quality of her skin, the shape of her mouth, her quick, intelligent mind. Lord, he even loved her temper.

"I hope you're going to do more than stare at me all night." She lifted her arms to encircle his neck. "I feel like I'm seventeen again, and I'm dying to be kissed. So kiss me, you toad."

Johnny laughed. Without doubt, he knew making love with Bailey Asher would be every bit as satisfying above the neck as below.

He bent his head toward hers and traced the edge of her upper lip with his tongue. He repeated the gentle touch, enjoying the gliding caress with an intensity that surprised him. His senses narrowed to the tip of his tongue as he dipped into the heat and softness of her mouth again and again, tasting and savoring until he felt every nerve-ending in his body come alive.

The first kiss seemed to go on forever. Suddenly, Johnny was aware that they had been touching and kissing with increasing fervor for some time, and his hand was sliding up her rib cage, over the cool silk she wore beneath her sweater. Then his hand was on her breast, and he could feel her nipple hot and erect upon the center of his palm.

"Okay?" he whispered against her lips, wanting to be sure she was with him every step of the way.

"Okay." She smiled crookedly, then molded her body to his, driving him wild.

Never had he wanted or needed a woman more, and judging from the way her body arched against him and the kitten-soft sounds purring in her throat, she wanted and needed him with a passion equal to his own.

"Johnny . . ." she cried out softly. She touched his face, and the contact was so electrifying, Johnny wouldn't have been surprised to see sparks and smoke.

They both fought to remove her sweater, then his. Her lacy white camisole soon followed. The rest of their clothing was rapidly dealt with and tossed aside as they touched and kissed their way into his bedroom.

They parted long enough for him to turn on the only lamp in the room and for her to toss back the linens. Then they stood looking at each other from opposite sides of the king-size bed.

Johnny drew in a short, ragged breath. She was beautiful, and she was his. "Bailey?"

"Yes?"

"Meet you in the middle?"

He saw no hesitation in her as she knelt on the mattress. He did the same.

When she met him halfway, he ran his hands over her shoulders and down her arms until his fingers laced with hers. Together, they sank down. For a long moment they lay side by side, simply enjoying the pleasure of being close and just looking at each other.

Johnny rose up on his elbow and slowly swept his hand over her hair. "Do you like having my hands on you?" he asked, watching her intently.

"I love your hands on me." She reached up and took the one stroking her hair. "They're gentle and warm." She drew his hand across her face and pressed her lips to his palm.

He smiled and lowered his mouth to her breasts. With everything male in him, he was aware of the yielding in her as he licked her swollen nipples, first one, then the other, lovingly, tenderly.

Bailey felt dazed and overwhelmed by her own fiercely rising passion, and she was swept away on a tide of emotion. Never in her life had she been so lacking in self-consciousness. Never had she wanted a man as much as she wanted Johnny. She eagerly reached for him, and he immediately covered her completely with his weight.

Her hands stroked over his body, and she thrilled to the perfect form and texture of him.

Each taut muscle and enticing angle, the width and breadth of his shoulders, the hard, flat planes of his chest, the subtle ripple of muscle on his stomach, the firmness of thighs and buttocks—all seemed to her a precise definition of ultimate masculinity.

He groaned her name, working his way up to kiss her throat. She was sure he could feel the throbbing of her pulse against his lips. Her heart was beating so fast. So was his.

She cradled his face between her hands and kissed his nose and each corner of his mouth, then trailed kisses along his jawline to his ear.

"I love you," she wanted to say but couldn't summon the clarity of mind to speak. She had fallen in love with his quiet strength, his compassion, the tranquillity in his eyes; with his body, his uncomplicated mind, the way he talked and walked; with his great capacity for patience, the way he simply loved life itself. . . .

He lifted his head and gazed down at her. "Bailey, I want you so much. If you want to stop, please tell me now."

"Don't stop." She moved her legs in restless invitation beneath the sweet weight of his thighs. "Don't ever stop. I trust you totally, completely."

He put a lot of love into a smile. "Thank you. I'll take good care of you."

"We'll take care of each other," she vowed with all her heart.

"I love you, Bailey," he whispered against her lips as he settled into the warmth between her legs.

He heard her sharp gasp and felt her go perfectly still beneath him. He closed his eyes, fearing he'd spoken his feeling too soon.

"Johnny?" Her fingers trembled on his face.

He set his jaw and lifted his head, half expecting to see panic in her expression. Instead, she was smiling so lovingly, he fell in love with her all over again.

"I'm very much in love with you too." The tenderness in her voice rippled over him in a surfeit of pleasure.

His breath caught. "That's the most beautiful thing anyone has ever said to me." He moved against her, and she arched her hips in response.

There's a place where wild and thoughtless passion dwells. Johnny discovered that wonderful place the moment he slipped inside her. He closed his eyes tightly, feeling as though he had suddenly been transformed into something better and more powerful. The feeling was intoxicating when combined with the emotions he'd guarded since the day she'd walked into his office.

They began to move together in a rhythm so fluid and sinuous, it was unlike anything he'd known before. He lost track of time, lost *himself* in the soft, silken heat of motion.

Every nerve in Bailey's body felt more sensitive than ever before. Each stroke Johnny took within her was so explosive with astonishing pleasure, pleasure that filled her completely and drove out every thought, until she clung mindlessly to him. With him she entered a palace of the heart and soul that she never wanted to leave.

When they both had reached a spiraling climax, they lay absolutely still, gazes locked together as firmly as their bodies. Silent messages passed between them, filled with a tenderness and love that neither could find the words to say aloud.

Johnny slowly withdrew from her and lay on his side, holding her close. It was good to feel so satiated, so content, after making love for the first time with the woman who held his very soul in the palm of her hand.

They lay for a time, neither speaking nor moving, until they gradually became aware of a chill creeping into the room. He reluctantly sat up, drew the covers over them, and switched off the light.

For a while they conversed intimately, exploring the years they had missed in each other's lives, and more was said with fewer words, until finally even their silences conveyed a rich communication.

Bailey was almost asleep when she felt Johnny's fingers trace her cheekbone. She opened her eyes and turned her head to look at him. In the pale moonlight his expression was as clear as the summer sky. In his eyes she saw more than passion. She saw wonder and a yearning so deep she could have wept from the sheer joy of it.

"You love me as much as I love you," he whispered. The gentle smile he gave her caught her heart and she smiled in return. "Marry me, Bailey Asher. We belong together."

Her smile trembled and faded. She tried to speak, but she was too moved by the tenderness and strength combined in this one man; too moved by the simple eloquence of his words and the emotion behind them. For a heartbeat she came close to surrendering to the shimmering promise of the life they could share.

Slow down, she warned herself, trying to calm her spiraling emotions. Marriage was not a commitment to be made lightly. "We'll talk about it in the morning," she told him softly.

He smiled and murmured something she couldn't decipher. His arm wound around her waist, and she turned to fit herself more closely to the warmth of his body. She lay awake for a long while, feeling the steady beat of Johnny's heart beneath her hand.

Bailey opened her eyes slowly to the dawn. One sleepy glance at the windows informed her that sometime during the night it had snowed again. The fresh layer of powder covering the trees and deck sparkled brilliantly in the morning light.

She lay unmoving for a moment, enjoying the feeling of being half-trapped by Johnny's bare leg, his arm a pleasant but heavy weight around her waist. Yawning drowsily, she turned her head on the pillow to look at him. He was still sleeping soundly. In that state of relaxation he looked very much like the little boy she'd first met at age five.

For some reason she was ridiculously pleased by that notion. "Toad face, I'm glad a part of you is still in there somewhere," she whispered, and smiled.

Then she remembered he had asked her to marry him. Her smile faded, and she regarded him gravely.

She didn't doubt that Johnny loved her. Nor did she doubt he would be a faithful husband, because he was an honorable man.

In a short time he had helped her break the

chains of her fear of physical and emotional intimacy. He'd even taught her the true meaning of
intimacy, that wonderful reciprocal expression of
feeling and thought. She knew he would always
wish to know her inner life, and he would always
want to share his.

Bailey was certain of all those things in her heart.
Yet she felt ill-equipped to cope with the idea of
marriage. It was simply too much, too soon. She'd
barely had time to adjust to the leap of faith she'd
taken in loving him.

Not thinking things through was one of her
faults. Marriage was a major commitment she
didn't want to rush into without carefully weigh-
ing all the factors involved.

She was confident Johnny would understand
she needed time to think things through.

An hour later Bailey discovered she was wrong.
Johnny didn't understand. Instead, he was incredulous and hurt.

She was dressed and sitting at the built-in table
in his kitchen, distressed at this sudden sharp rift
she'd caused between them. He was pacing the
floor, his arms crossed over his chest, a scowl on
his face.

"You're upset," she said.

"Hell yes, I'm upset." He stopped pacing.
"You're panicking. Pushing me away, because I
got too close to you last night."

"No, that's not it at all."

"Do you love me, Bailey?"

"Yes, I do."

"Then what's the problem?" He sat down across

from her. Chin in hand, he regarded her intently. She felt as though he was trying to crawl inside her mind to see what made her tick.

She ran her fingers through her bangs, searching for the words to adequately express her feelings. "Emotional overload and more changes in my life than I've had time to fully understand." She smiled wryly and shook her head.

"Originally, I came to Profitt simply as a means of changing the direction of my career. I didn't expect to go through so many changes in my personal life. But I have. I didn't expect to rediscover my best friend and fall in love with him. But I have. You've helped me conquer my fears and restored my faith in the common decency of human beings. That's a lot of changes to cope with in such a short time. Marrying you will bring about even more, and I have to be certain I want to make those changes."

Silence filled the room, the kind of silence that followed a tornado's deadly sound and fury. Then Johnny smiled, but there was no humor in the thin curve of his mouth.

"Part of those changes you're so concerned about involves the job. The work here isn't challenging enough for you, is it?"

Bailey's calm faltered. "Yes. That is one of the things I need time to think about."

"How much time?"

"A day, weeks, months." She shrugged helplessly. "I honestly don't know how much time it will take."

He looked at her for the longest moment of her life. She watched one emotion after another shadow his eyes until all color and warmth seemed to drain from him. Only a great effort of will kept her from caving in to the unhappiness so clearly reflected in his expression.

"I'm trying to do what's right for both of us, Johnny. For once I'm going to think carefully before rushing such an important decision." She smiled ruefully. "You've taught me the wisdom of that."

Johnny remained silent, watching her with those shadowed eyes. Then he made an odd, almost regretful gesture. "I hope teaching you that lesson doesn't turn out to be the worst mistake of my life."

Johnny drove Bailey to her aunt's house. After seeing her to the door, he returned to his car and backed out of Mrs. Hoover's driveway. Then, because he suddenly knew he didn't want to go home, he drove into his parents' driveway. They weren't home, he brilliantly deduced from the absence of their vehicle, so they certainly wouldn't mind him hanging around to mope for a while.

He felt that he was losing Bailey.

That was illogical, of course. She hadn't refused to marry him. Just requested time to think it over.

As her best friend, he would advise her to do just that. Think carefully. Be reasonable. Be smart.

But as her lover and the man who wanted to marry her, he thought that was stinky advice.

Johnny believed she loved him, because he was dead certain lust hadn't been her prime motivation for going home with him last night. Though lust had been a great bonus.

Glancing up at her bedroom window, he considered the real reason he felt that he was losing her.

He was afraid.

Afraid she would decide she couldn't be happy living in a little country town.

Afraid she was too bright, too ambitious, and too restless to be happy indefinitely with her job as the sheriff's detective.

Whatever she decided, she'd have to follow her heart both professionally and personally. He just hoped she didn't wind up breaking his.

Johnny drummed his fingers on the steering wheel. He needed something to do, something physical, to keep his mind occupied and his frustration level in control. But what?

He still didn't want to go home. There, he would be constantly reminded of Bailey every time he looked at the sofa and chairs she'd chosen for his living room, every time he looked at his unmade bed.

His gaze lit upon his parents' garage. Mom had been nagging him for months to come over and clean it out, but he'd been putting it off in favor of his carpentry work in his own house.

"Guess my misfortune is your good luck, Ma," he muttered, and got out of his car.

# *Eleven*

---

Johnny's Blazer was parked next door when Bailey left the house to go for a drive to sort out her tangled emotions. Upon her return several hours later, she was disappointed to see the Blazer was no longer there.

Disappointed because she'd relentlessly searched her soul and had reached some startling conclusions. She had hoped he would still be there, because she needed to talk to her best friend.

The phone was ringing as she entered the house through the back door. Hoping it was Johnny, she raced across the kitchen and grabbed the receiver. "Hello!"

"Detective Asher, I'm real sorry to bother you." She recognized Deputy Adkins's grumbling baritone voice. "I'm down at the station. The sheriff's done lost his mind. Ranting and raving. I don't know what to do. Never seen him act so crazy."

Her heart jumped up into her throat. "My God! What's going on?"

"He's done arrested his own parents, his uncle, and your aunt, that's what's going on. He's got 'em all fingerprinted, booked, and locked up tighter than Cole Wan's Bar on Sunday morning. I think you better get down here quick."

Bailey hung up the phone and dashed out the door.

She was scared and confused by the time she reached the station house.

Determined not to show it, Bailey forced herself to enter the building sedately. She even managed a jaunty little wave and a smile for the dispatcher as she passed by the glass window of the communications area.

Going down the corridor, she saw Deputy Adkins and another weekend deputy she'd met only once. Both men had an ear pressed against the closed outer-chamber of the sheriff's office. It took no brilliant detective work to guess where Johnny was holed up.

"Is he breaking up the furniture, boys?" she asked dryly, startling the officers, who hadn't heard her approach.

The weekend deputy looked embarrassed and kept silent.

Deputy Adkins was obviously made of sterner stuff, because he grinned. "Nope. It's quiet as Tucker's Funeral Parlor in there."

"I imagine you both can find something to do somewhere else?" She gave each of them a look that indicated they shouldn't argue.

The deputy caved in immediately and took off in the direction from which Bailey had just come.

Adkins wasn't as easily moved. "Imagine I could use a cup of coffee about now," he drawled. He saluted her and strolled down the corridor at a much more leisurely pace than his fellow officer.

Bailey took a deep breath to quiet her nerves, then she opened the door and breezed through the administrative assistant's antechamber. She didn't bother knocking before she walked into Johnny's office.

"Get lost," he growled. At least, she thought that's what he'd said. It was hard to tell because his voice was so muffled. He was sitting at his desk, bent over, face down on the desktop, arms curved around his head.

"Taking a little nap?" She shut the door behind her and leaned back against it for support.

He slowly raised his head, and she felt a moment's panic rise up in her throat. Pure rage blazed in his eyes, and his expression was grim. "They're all criminals."

"Who?" She stepped farther into the room.

"My whole damn family and your aunt, that's who." He was practically shaking.

Bailey stared at him and dropped down in the chair closest to him. "Tell me what's going on."

Johnny leaned forward and picked up a small spiral notebook from the desktop. "I found this hidden in my parents' garage along with stolen VCRs and jewelry." He tossed it to her. "Go ahead. Take a look. Makes real interesting reading."

"I don't believe it."

"I've got confessions."

Bailey opened the notebook. As she scanned the

pages, he explained the whole scheme to her in great detail, growing more agitated and angry with every breath.

When he finished by telling her what he intended to do, she was stunned by their families' misguided objectives and by Johnny's iron determination to carry out the letter of the law against all four of them.

They were both silent for an eternal moment.

Finally, Bailey sighed and shook her head. "Well, they certainly got carried away in their desire to get us married. But it sounds like the only real crime they committed was falsely reporting criminal incidents and conspiring to keep us busy chasing down a nonexistent Peeping Tom."

"I don't care," he said stubbornly. "I'm throwing the book at them."

"Then you'll have to bring charges against half the senior citizens in Profitt," she pointed out. "Come election time, nobody will want to vote for the man who put their parents and grandparents in jail for malicious mischief."

"So what? I don't care if they vote me out. I'm going to do the right thing."

She got up, walking around the desk to put her arms across his shoulders. His muscles felt tight beneath her hands. "I care. If you lose your office, the whole county loses. You're the best man for the job, Sheriff Charm. Hart's Law might not work in a city, but it works here. And if you lose your job . . ." Her voice trailed off.

This wasn't exactly the time and place she would have chosen to discuss with him the decisions she'd made. She forged ahead anyway. "If you lose your job, how are you going to support me and our children in the fashion in which we intend to become accustomed?"

Johnny couldn't have been more startled if she had smacked him with a two-by-four. "You're going to marry me?"

"You bet."

"Why?" he asked, suspicion heavy in his voice.

She smiled. "Because I love you, toad. And because I've come to like being a small-town law officer. A very wise, *compassionate* sheriff taught me the importance of the *spirit* of the law. I like the less stressful way of life and the rewarding feeling that comes from the good wishes of the public."

"I love you, too, brat." He pulled her down onto his lap and hugged her tight.

Silence reigned between them again, a silence as comfortable as a dear and old friend.

"If you ever find that you're unhappy here," Johnny said finally, "if you have a change of heart about your career, I'll go wherever you want." He leaned back to meet her gaze, and she knew he meant every word.

"Johnny—"

"Let me finish. I know I'd never fit in with a big-city police force, but I'd move in a minute if that's what you want."

"You hate cities!"

"I'd live in one with you. I could coach high school football or work on my master's degree in psychology. I—"

Bailey stopped his rapid flow of words with her mouth. The depth of his love for her touched her soul.

"We're staying here right in Profitt," she said firmly, when they broke apart to breathe.

"Okay." His smile was warmer than a Fourth of July morning.

"And we're going to let our families out of jail."

He shook his head. "No way. I don't approve of what they did."

"Yes way. Neither do I." She lifted her chin and stared at him stubbornly. "We're going to let Judge Wilkins sentence our wayward senior citizens to however many hours of community-service work he feels is suitable punishment."

"All right," Johnny said grudgingly. "You win. After all, their intent wasn't criminal but conjugal. I guess that should earn them some leniency."

She grinned. "Let's go let the jailbirds out."

He stopped her from rising, keeping his arms firmly locked around her waist. "Let 'em sleep on it for a while. I have business to take care of."

"Oh? And what might that be, Sheriff Charm?"

Johnny grinned mischievously. He stood up and set her on the desk. "Laying down the law with a fiery redhead who stole my heart."

As he urged her to lie back on the desk, Bailey didn't give him a bit of trouble. A dose of Hart's Law was just what she needed.

# THE EDITOR'S CORNER

Next month LOVESWEPT presents an Easter parade of six fabulous romances. Not even April showers can douse the terrific mood you'll be in after reading each and every one of these treasures.

The hero of Susan Connell's new LOVESWEPT, #606, is truly **SOME KIND OF WONDERFUL**. As mysterious and exciting as the Greek islands he calls home, Alex Stoner is like a gorgeous god whose mouth promises pagan pleasures. He's also a cool businessman who never lets a woman get close. But prim and proper Sandy Patterson, widow of his college roommate, is unlike any he's ever known, and he sets out to make her ache for his own brand of passion. Susan takes you on a roller coaster of emotion with this romance.

Kay Hooper continues her MEN OF MYSTERIES PAST series with **HUNTING THE WOLFE**, LOVESWEPT #607. Security expert Wolfe Nickerson appeared in the first book in the series, **THE TOUCH OF MAX**, LOVESWEPT #595, and in this new novel, he almost finds himself bested by a pint-sized computer programmer. Storm Tremaine blows into his life like a force of nature, promising him the chase of his life . . . and hinting she's fast enough to catch him! When he surrenders to her womanly charms, he doesn't know that Storm holds a secret . . . a secret that could forever destroy his trust. Kay is at her best with this terrific love story.

**BREATHLESS,** LOVESWEPT #608 by Diane Persh-ing, is how Hollis Blake feels when Tony Stellini walks into her gift shop. The tall, dark, and sensuous lawyer makes the air sizzle with his wildfire energy, and for the first time Hollis longs to taste every pleasure she's never had, pursue all the dreams she's been denied. Her innocence stirs an overpowering desire in Tony, but he senses that with this untouched beauty, he has to take it one slow, delicious step at a time. This is a romance to relish, a treat from Diane.

Linda Cajio begins **DANCING IN THE DARK,** LOVE-SWEPT #609, with an eye-opening scene in which the hero is engaged in a sacred ceremony and dancing naked in the woods! Jake Halford feels a little silly performing the men's movement ritual, but Charity Brown feels downright embarrassed at catching him at it. How can she ever work with her company's new vice president without remembering the thrilling sight of his muscles and power? The way Linda has these two learning how to mix business and pleasure is a pure delight.

**HANNAH'S HUNK,** LOVESWEPT #610 by Sandra Chastain, is nothing less than a sexy rebel with a southern drawl . . . and an ex-con whom Hannah Clendening "kidnaps" so he could pose for the cover of her Fantasy Romance. Dan Bailey agrees, but only if Hannah plays the heroine and he gets to kiss her. When desire flares between them like a force field, neither believes that what they feel could last. Of course Sandra, with her usual wit and charm, makes sure there's a happily ever after for this unusual couple.

Finally, there's **THE TROUBLE WITH MAGIC,** LOVE-SWEPT #611 by Mary Kay McComas. Harriet Wheaton has an outrageous plan to keep Payton Dunsmore from foreclosing on the great manor house on Jovette Island. Marooning them there, she tells him that she's trying to fulfill the old legend of enemies meeting on Jovette and falling in love! Payton's furious at first, but he soon succumbs to the enchantment of the island . . . and Harriet herself. Mary Kay delivers pure magic with this marvelous romance.

On sale this month from FANFARE are four outstanding novels. If you missed **TEMPERATURES RISING** by blockbuster author Sandra Brown when it first came out, now's your chance to grab a copy of this wonderfully evocative love story. Chantal duPont tells herself that she needs Scout Ritland only to build a much-needed bridge on the South Pacific island she calls home. And when the time comes for him to leave, she must make the painful decision of letting him go—or risking everything by taking a chance on love.

From beloved author Rosanne Bittner comes **OUTLAW HEARTS,** a stirring new novel of heart-stopping danger and burning desire. At twenty, Miranda Hayes has known more than her share of heartache and loss. Then she clashes with the notorious gunslinger Jake Harkner, a hard-hearted loner with a price on his head, and finds within herself a deep well of courage . . . and feelings of desire she's never known before.

Fanfare is proud to publish **THE LAST HIGHWAYMAN,** the first historical romance by Katherine O'Neal, a truly exciting new voice in women's fiction. In this delectable action-packed novel, Christina has money, power, and position, but she has never known reckless passion, never found enduring love . . . until she is kidnapped by a dangerously handsome bandit who needs her to heal his tormented soul.

In the bestselling tradition of Danielle Steel, **CONFI-DENCES** by Penny Hayden is a warm, deeply moving novel about four "thirty-something" mothers whose lives are interwoven by a long-held secret—a secret that could now save the life of a seventeen-year-old boy dying of leukemia.

Also available now in the hardcover edition from Double-day is **MASK OF NIGHT** by Lois Wolfe, a stunning historical novel of romantic suspense. When an actress and a cattle rancher join forces against a diabolical villain, the result is an unforgettable story of love and ven-geance.

Happy reading!

With warmest wishes,

*Nita Taublib*

Nita Taublib
Associate Publisher
LOVESWEPT and FANFARE

# OFFICIAL RULES TO WINNERS CLASSIC SWEEPSTAKES

No Purchase necessary. To enter the sweepstakes follow instructions found elsewhere in this offer. You can also enter the sweepstakes by hand printing your name, address, city, state and zip code on a 3" x 5" piece of paper and mailing it to: Winners Classic Sweepstakes, P.O. Box 785, Gibbstown, NJ 08027. Mail each entry separately. Sweepstakes begins 12/1/91. Entries must be received by 6/1/93. Some presentations of this sweepstakes may feature a deadline for the Early Bird prize. If the offer you receive does, then to be eligible for the Early Bird prize your entry must be received according to the Early Bird date specified. Not responsible for lost, late, damaged, misdirected, illegible or postage due mail. Mechanically reproduced entries are not eligible. All entries become property of the sponsor and will not be returned.

Prize Selection/Validations: Winners will be selected in random drawings on or about 7/30/93, by VENTURA ASSOCIATES, INC., an independent judging organization whose decisions are final. Odds of winning are determined by total number of entries received. Circulation of this sweepstakes is estimated not to exceed 200 million. Entrants need not be present to win. All prizes are guaranteed to be awarded and delivered to winners. Winners will be notified by mail and may be required to complete an affidavit of eligibility and release of liability which must be returned within 14 days of date of notification or alternate winners will be selected. Any guest of a trip winner will also be required to execute a release of liability. Any prize notification letter or any prize returned to a participating sponsor, Bantam Doubleday Dell Publishing Group, Inc., its participating divisions or subsidiaries, or VENTURA ASSOCIATES, INC. as undeliverable will be awarded to an alternate winner. Prizes are not transferable. No multiple prize winners except as may be necessary due to unavailability, in which case a prize of equal or greater value will be awarded. Prizes will be awarded approximately 90 days after the drawing. All taxes, automobile license and registration fees, if applicable, are the sole responsibility of the winners. Entry constitutes permission (except where prohibited) to use winners' names and likenesses for publicity purposes without further or other compensation.

Participation: This sweepstakes is open to residents of the United States and Canada, except for the province of Quebec. This sweepstakes is sponsored by Bantam Doubleday Dell Publishing Group, Inc. (BDD), 666 Fifth Avenue, New York, NY 10103. Versions of this sweepstakes with different graphics will be offered in conjunction with various solicitations or promotions by different subsidiaries and divisions of BDD. Employees and their families of BDD, its division, subsidiaries, advertising agencies, and VENTURA ASSOCIATES, INC., are not eligible.

Canadian residents, in order to win, must first correctly answer a time limited arithmetical skill testing question. Void in Quebec and wherever prohibited or restricted by law. Subject to all federal, state, local and provincial laws and regulations.

Prizes: The following values for prizes are determined by the manufacturers' suggested retail prices or by what these items are currently known to be selling for at the time this offer was published. Approximate retail values include handling and delivery of prizes. Estimated maximum retail value of prizes: 1 Grand Prize ($27,500 if merchandise or $25,000 Cash); 1 First Prize ($3,000); 5 Second Prizes ($400 each); 35 Third Prizes ($100 each); 1,000 Fourth Prizes ($9.00 each); 1 Early Bird Prize ($5,000); Total approximate maximum retail value is $50,000. Winners will have the option of selecting any prize offered at level won. Automobile winner must have a valid driver's license at the time the car is awarded. Trips are subject to space and departure availability. Certain black-out dates may apply. Travel must be completed within one year from the time the prize is awarded. Minors must be accompanied by an adult. Prizes won by minors will be awarded in the name of parent or legal guardian.

For a list of Major Prize Winners (available after 7/30/93): send a self-addressed, stamped envelope entirely separate from your entry to: Winners Classic Sweepstakes Winners, P.O. Box 825, Gibbstown, NJ 08027. Requests must be received by 6/1/93. DO NOT SEND ANY OTHER CORRESPONDENCE TO THIS P.O. BOX.

# Bestselling Women's Fiction

## Sandra Brown

| | | |
|---|---|---|
| _____ | 29783-X A WHOLE NEW LIGHT | $5.99/6.99 in Canada |
| _____ | 29500-4 TEXAS! SAGE | $5.99/6.99 |
| _____ | 29085-1 22 INDIGO PLACE | $4.50/5.50 |
| _____ | 28990-X TEXAS! CHASE | $5.99/6.99 |
| _____ | 28951-9 TEXAS! LUCKY | $5.99/6.99 |

## Amanda Quick

| | | |
|---|---|---|
| _____ | 29316-8 RAVISHED | $4.99/5.99 |
| _____ | 29315-X RECKLESS | $5.99/6.99 |
| _____ | 29325-7 RENDEZVOUS | $4.99/5.99 |
| _____ | 28932-2 SCANDAL | $4.95/5.95 |
| _____ | 28354-5 SEDUCTION | $4.99/5.99 |
| _____ | 28594-7 SURRENDER | $5.99/6.99 |

## Nora Roberts

| | | |
|---|---|---|
| _____ | 29490-3 DIVINE EVIL | $5.99/6.99 |
| _____ | 29597-7 CARNAL INNOCENCE | $5.50/6.50 |
| _____ | 29078-9 GENUINE LIES | $4.99/5.99 |
| _____ | 28578-5 PUBLIC SECRETS | $4.95/5.95 |
| _____ | 26461-3 HOT ICE | $4.99/5.99 |
| _____ | 26574-1 SACRED SINS | $5.50/6.50 |
| _____ | 27859-2 SWEET REVENGE | $5.50/6.50 |
| _____ | 27283-7 BRAZEN VIRTUE | $4.99/5.99 |

## Iris Johansen

| | | |
|---|---|---|
| _____ | 29968-9 THE TIGER PRINCE | $5.50/6.50 |
| _____ | 29871-2 LAST BRIDGE HOME | $4.50/5.50 |
| _____ | 29604-3 THE GOLDEN BARBARIAN | $4.99/5.99 |
| _____ | 29244-7 REAP THE WIND | $4.99/5.99 |
| _____ | 29032-0 STORM WINDS | $4.99/5.99 |
| _____ | 28855-5 THE WIND DANCER | $4.95/5.95 |

**Ask for these titles at your bookstore or use this page to order.**

Please send me the books I have checked above. I am enclosing $ _____ (add $2.50 to cover postage and handling). Send check or money order, no cash or C. O. D.'s please.

Mr./ Ms. _____

Address _____

City/ State/ Zip _____

Send order to: Bantam Books, Dept. FN 16, 2451 S. Wolf Road, Des Plaines, IL 60018
Please allow four to six weeks for delivery.
Prices and availability subject to change without notice.

FN 16 -3/93